THE OT

Jon Neal has a Master of Arts in Writing from Swinburne University. His poems and short stories have been published in multiple anthologies, and he was runner up in the 2010 Sydney Mardi Gras short story competition. His debut short novel '*A Twin Room*' was published in 2022 and reached number 1 in its Amazon category. He lives with his partner in Sussex.

The Other Path

JON NEAL

For Kate. Who wanted a mystery.

CHAPTER ONE

He was nothing more than a shape. A dark silhouette against the moonlit snow.

His drunken steps slid and stumbled on the slippery ground making him fall over and pull himself back up again repeatedly.

Even from such a deliberate distance, it was obvious that he was unaware of his wider surroundings. Too focused on trying to stay upright and get home to consider that he might be being followed. Who would be around at a time like this in such a quiet place?

He had paused now. Right by the pond.

He swayed.

Now was the perfect opportunity. Almost too good to be true.

He was looking up at the stars. Perhaps he was wondering at how they'd aligned. But not for him. Not in that moment.

He wouldn't have known.

The end came quick, with the blackness descending before he even saw it approach.

*

The next morning, Bridget Heywood was preoccupied. However optimistic she tried to be she couldn't help thinking of her old life. A life in which she'd complained about being too busy, too stressed, too underpaid.

She shivered.

Remembering that other version of herself was too painful. So far removed from the cold reality of where she was now.

Joyce, sat in her chair in the corner, straightened her back and watched intently. Bridget wondered whether she should offer to find her a blanket. To wrap around her shoulders or drape across her knees. A hot water bottle, perhaps?

The small single pane windows had, she noticed in horror, ice on the *inside* of them. It was primitive. Something of the Victorian novel about it. Dark and dingy.

'Patrick's worried about the livestock,' she said.

'Those animals don't feel the cold. They're tough beasts. Nature's made them strong.'

Bridget thought Joyce could've been referring to herself. Her dismissive words stung. Would they always be the inexperienced ones? What difference would approval make anyhow?

How Bridget longed to throw caution to the wind. To occasionally go to the shops or indulge in reading a good book. To be anywhere but here. Tied to the daily machinations of rural life.

Here everything was regimented. Routines, dictated by seasons and traditions, to be strictly adhered to. A daily running order that couldn't be changed.

Other women, Bridget supposed, might be stronger. Imposing their will. Unafraid to shake things up. But other women hadn't been in her position. What choice had she had?

A floorboard squeaked. The sound over their heads intruded upon them. Bridget anticipated an observation from Joyce. And yet this morning no words came. Just an uneasy silence. Which Bridget didn't know was better or worse.

She busied herself with a cloth about the kitchen. The chores, she'd learnt, were both a burden and distraction. She'd always thought of herself as a hard worker until they'd moved in. This place required a level of energy and resolve she never knew she had.

All a matter of perspective.

Bridget glanced at her mute companion. Her ruddy complexion and wiry grey hair spoke of a lifetime's toil. Despite still being a strong woman, even she couldn't have held the farm together alone. It was so unlike her not to be voicing opinions. For all her frustration at Joyce's cantankerous ways, the faraway look in her watery eyes this morning concerned her.

'Are you feeling unwell?' Bridget ventured.

The old woman frowned. 'Unwell?'

Bridget felt brave. 'You just seem quiet this morning. A little out of sorts?'

Joyce folded her hands in her lap. She raised her whiskery chin like an obstinate child. The meaning of the gesture was unclear. Was she offended by Bridget's concern? Or was there something else troubling her?

To Bridget, it looked like a petulant sulk. She may as well have stuck out her bottom lip.

Bridget shrugged and resumed her domestic duties. It was probably just another chapter in the dance they'd played since moving in. A tip-toe dance in which they tried to avoid direct confrontation. Skirting around the land mines. A passive aggressive series of manoeuvres in which change sat uncomfortably.

Downlands Farm nestled in a remote hollow of the Sussex countryside. A small holding, with several acres. Its farmhouse was ragged, skirted by ramshackle outbuildings and rusty agricultural paraphernalia. It sat at the foot of the rolling downs. The expanse of hills rose up so high around it that at this time of year the sun barely lifted above them.

Bridget frequently thought about how unprepared she'd been. She'd known Downlands Farm, of course; it'd always been in Patrick's blood. But the enormity of actually *living* there was something else entirely. The wrench of it, season through season, had felt like her very being had been uprooted.

Again, what choice had there been?

The question plagued her: Had there been another way?

Too late now. They'd made their choices. This maze she now found herself in was of their own doing.

She checked the range again, not entirely convinced that it was still alight, only to discover that a flame still flickered within.

How had Joyce and her late husband Doug done it for all those years? Bridget remembered him being

4

strong as an ox. The couple had seemed to have the constitution for it. Hardy and resilient. Yet despite that dogged determination, even Doug hadn't been able to defeat the aggression of the virus. To become another statistic in a pandemic.

Bridget didn't like to think of that time. It raised memories and emotions that she didn't know how to handle. It marked a crossroads between an old life and a new one. An absolute change of direction.

Footsteps sounded on the staircase.

Bridget's daughter Imogen appeared at the door like a ghost. An apparition in black. Her hair hung forlornly about her shoulders. The bohemian dress she wore sat uneasily upon her slender frame. Bridget noticed that the black eyeliner had been drawn on thicker this morning. At nineteen, Imogen was drifting. Still to find her way.

'Earth to Mum?'

'Yes?' said Bridget.

'Did you hear what I said to you?'

'I wasn't listening, sorry.'

Imogen sighed. 'I said, it's George. He's not replying to my texts.'

'He was a bit worse for wear at the party.'

'It was hardly what you'd call a party. Just a few drinks at the pub.'

All a matter of perspective, Bridget thought. What constituted a party in the eyes of a teenager was very different from her own thoughts these days.

'Did he misbehave?' Joyce asked, directing the question at her granddaughter.

Bridget, as was her wont, fought the urge to defend her brother.

'George was just George,' said Imogen. There was an undeniable affection between grandmother and grandchild. The vastness in years that separated them somehow spared them the friction that Bridget herself often perceived. They almost looked on one another as entirely different species. Their aloof kinship sometimes felt conspiratorial. Clinging to one another in the face of adversity. Finding strength in numbers.

'How many times have you messaged him?' Bridget asked.

'Loads. He usually replies.'

Bridget looked at the clock. It was still very early by George's standards.

The kitchen walls loomed down on her. Joyce's eyes bore into her. Bridget knew how Joyce felt about George. She'd said her piece on numerous occasions.

'Perhaps I'll walk over to see him. Just to make sure that he has supplies.'

Bridget noticed Joyce fidget. It looked as if she was sitting on un-said words. Trying to contain herself.

'Do you want to come with me?' Bridget asked Imogen.

'Not this morning. I'm going to stay in the warm.'

It troubled Bridget that her daughter had yet to find a purpose. Imogen had always been a free spirit. They'd encouraged that in her. Not thinking where that would leave her as an adult in the working world. She had dreams. But dreams, Bridget knew, wouldn't put a roof over her head or food on the table.

Bridget left Imogen and Joyce to their quiet little bond. She pulled on her wellington boots and put on a coat, scarf and gloves. As she opened the door, sunlight hit the snowy landscape. She raised her hand above her eyes and squinted.

Snow had begun to fall early yesterday morning. What started as a few wispy flakes had soon escalated into a heavy downfall.

'Off out?'

It was Patrick. He strode towards her holding a bucket for feeding the animals.

'Just going to George's.'

'To check up on him? Make sure he's ok?' said Patrick, adding: 'That was quite some performance he put in last night.'

Bridget didn't want a confrontation this morning. She didn't want to trawl through it all again.

'He's my brother.'

'Let's not do this today, eh?'

'Let's not.'

Plumes of exasperated vapour escaped her mouth. She saw her breath rise before her.

'Just take care. Be careful. The snow has drifted in places. It came down so hard and unexpectedly that the gritting lorry didn't get a chance to come through. They always prioritise the towns first.'

'So the road into Littleworth is unpassable?'

'Completely cut off. We were right last night. We must've been isolated by midday. No-one coming in. No-one going out.'

A gust of icy wind lifted flurries from the ground.

The farmyard glittered. Light glinted off icicles.

A community trapped in its very own snow globe.

Bridget set off. Her boots trudged heavily in the snow. What was only a short walk had the air of an intrepid voyage. She felt like an explorer on a journey into a bleak unknown wilderness, fascinated that her surrounds could be transformed by a blanket of snow. She marvelled at how it lay upon branches and on the tops of the stone walls.

At the gates of Downlands Farm, she took a moment to absorb the scene. It looked like a sentimental Christmas card.

Littleworth was best described as a hamlet. Too small to really be considered a village, although there was a traditional sign carved out of wood that stood on a small triangle of turf opposite the local pub, The Plough. The place was nothing more than a small cluster of properties.

Setting forth again, Bridget saw a familiar figure silhouetted against the whiteness.

'Ursula!'

The woman turned. But before she'd had a chance to compose her features, Bridget swore she'd seen a look of anxiety upon her face. She was pale, and on registering Bridget's presence her expression settled quickly into an amicable painted smile.

'I don't remember us having snow like this for decades,' she said. 'Quentin and I wondered whether the post might still get delivered.'

'I doubt it. The roads look completely blocked.'

'It's not what The Plough needs, is it? Another blow

to their business.'

'They'll have to rely on summer trade.'

Ursula looked doubtful. She and her partner Quentin represented the old guard. Apparently, they'd lived at Flint Cottage for eternity. A quintessential abode with a picket fence where in summer roses rambled around the front porch.

'Are you going to see George?' Ursula asked. She and George had struck up a somewhat unlikely friendship. Although, Bridget admitted, when it came to George nothing was ever really unlikely. 'I should think he's got a headache this morning.' Ursula's eyes twinkled. There was approval there. Or something.

It'd always been the case. George liked to be the topic of conversation.

'I'm just going to check that he's got something in his fridge. The weather's probably taken him by surprise.'

Ursula laughed. 'You're a good sister.'

Bridget wasn't sure about that.

They bid farewell to one another. Ursula retreated cautiously up her treacherous front path and slipped away behind the door of Flint Cottage.

Bridget suddenly felt very alone.

A silence descended. The snow muffled any sound. The absence of any birdsong gave a sombre sense of foreboding. Above her, ominous clouds scudded across the sky. They looked heavy. They covered the sun and Littleworth grew shadowy and dark.

Just beyond Flint Cottage was the laneway which led down to Riplingham Barn. A pitted track lined with tall hedgerows and trees, completely setback from the road, entirely concealed and private. Hidden from view.

At first glance, the barn appeared as it always did with its timber frame and large windows. An impressive façade of both traditional and modern.

Drawing closer, however, something didn't feel right.

Bridget would wonder later whether she might call it intuition. Or had she known already? There was something just not *right*.

Panic rose within her. Her heart raced. All the fears she'd ever had for him. All the sleepless nights that she, his big sister, might fail to protect him. It was irrational, and yet entirely real.

It was as if she'd known before she'd seen.

Against the whiteness of the snow, there in the large ornamental pond, was an incongruous patch of red.

Bridget took a moment to comprehend what it was. To begin with, just a passing curiosity. Then as she drew nearer the horror struck. A terrible realisation.

George's coat. And he was still wearing it. Face down in the frozen pond.

'George?' her voice cracked. 'George!'

It was all the things she'd ever feared. How she always dreaded it would end. An untimely, and some would say, inevitable demise.

CHAPTER TWO

(i)

TRIBUTES TO LITTLEWORTH MAN WHO DIED AFTER ACCIDENT

Family and friends of a man who died after a fall outside his Littleworth home have paid tribute to a 'unique and special' person.

George Thorpe, aged 35, was found dead at his home, Riplingham Barn, on the morning of 9th January sparking a police investigation.

But officers ruled that there was no foul play and the case was passed to the coroner for East Sussex who opened an inquest in Lewes. The verdict of this inquest has been listed as 'death consistent with head injury following accidental fall.'

(ii)

Summer brought a new beginning and technicolour to Downlands Farm. The paddocks shone a lush emerald green. Abundant hedgerows hummed with insects. Birds swooped delighted in the sky.

Patrick returned from the fields to find Bridget pegging out the laundry. The sheets billowed in the soft breeze.

'Let me help you,' he said.

Bridget looked tired. The last six months had taken their toll.

'There's a piece in the newspaper about the inquest,' she said quietly as if nervous that they might be overheard.

'Anything new?'

'No. Just the facts.'

'I suppose that's that then. Like a line's been drawn underneath it.'

Bridget clutched the damp laundry. 'It didn't feel like the story was about him. To see it outlined so plainly in black and white. It was so cold. So clinical.'

Patrick understood. Many times he'd felt as if they'd stepped into someone else's life. A twist of fate. Thrust into an alien world of investigations and unfathomable terminology.

'We knew the outcome.'

Sometimes he feared it wasn't the outcome she wanted. There was no justice in a verdict of accidental death or misadventure. Just a vague cloud hanging over circumstances and George's character.

'It was just the seeing it in print. Something so private as death cast out to the public for the whole word to see. Just for a few column inches in the news.'

Patrick wondered who in Littleworth would read it. There was probably a copy lying about at The Plough.

He had half a mind to go and see.

'I suppose that really is the end of it then,' said Patrick. Bridget's brooding silence suggested that he'd said the wrong thing. 'I meant the end of the legalities. Not the end of forgetting George.'

Bridget's shoulders slumped. 'Do you think we'll always be walking on eggshells? Skirting around uncomfortable conversations?'

She wasn't just referring to the death of her brother. Patrick knew that.

'Aren't things getting better?' he said. 'Don't things look just that little bit more hopeful in the sunshine?'

'I'm not sure I'm ready to let go of the past yet.'

'Nobody's forcing you to.'

He wanted to make it better. If only they could go back in time, perhaps the path that had led them here might look different.

'You know I haven't found it easy. None of it.'

Her sweeping statement held innumerable possibilities. There were so many challenges littered along the way. They'd become tangled like bindweed. Almost impossible to see where one ended and another began.

Patrick didn't like it when she spoke this way. It made him nervous that she still held him responsible.

'The battles have worn me out,' said Bridget. He supposed she was referring to Joyce whose opinions had not quietened or softened. An ever-present tug-of-war over territory.

'We can win the war,' he said. 'I *know* we can.'

It pained him to think of their old life. A time when

they'd spoken honestly with one another. If only they didn't speak to one another now in this coded language. This cryptic way of communicating that never got to the crux of the matter. Too afraid of opening Pandora's box.

'What if it's *not* over?'

Patrick didn't know what she meant. 'The outcome of the inquest is final. We have to accept that.'

Bridget looked doubtful. He sensed that she didn't want to let it go. That she'd found some unhealthy solace in picking at the scab.

'Isn't it always going to hang over us? Like some horrible dark cloud?'

The past can never be escaped. He felt that all too keenly.

Patrick worried that his determination to start looking to the future might not be shared as strongly by his wife.

A black bird appeared and perched on the wall. It sang with such joy that it stopped them in their tracks for a moment. His melody trilled. Then he leapt away in a flurry of little wings.

'A visitor from the other side?' Bridget said.

'Very possibly.'

They shook the sheets between them. The pillowcases were next. It was all part of the new routine. One that Patrick secretly hoped might provide Bridget with a feeling of purpose and accomplishment, but feared only served as another reminder of the person she'd once been.

*

Stanley Messina pulled on the hand brake and turned off the engine.

He'd looked at Littleworth on the map but seeing it in person brought the geography of the place to life. To the right of him stood the traditional pub. Parasols up on wooden tables. Ahead lay what looked like agricultural land with a farmhouse on its slope. Whilst on his left, across the road, stood a chocolate box cottage.

Stanley lifted the printed instructions from the passenger seat and dialled the number listed. She was quick to answer. She'd been expecting him. She would be right with him.

He got out of the car and placed the folded newspaper beneath his arm. He wanted to make sure that it was immediately visible to her.

The sun beat down upon him.

A figure approached from the direction of the farmhouse. She wore dungarees. Her hair tied in a ponytail. She strode with purpose and momentum. In Stanley's experience, first impressions counted. They couldn't always be relied upon, but they often said a lot about a person. She gave him a wave. The welcome looked warm and genuine.

'I'm Bridget,' she said, extending her hand to him. 'You must be Mr Messina?'

So it was her. The dead man's sister.

'Please, call me Stanley.'

They shook hands.

'You found us okay?'

'Your directions were very clear.'

Her eyes alighted, as hoped, on the printed pages. He tried to judge her reaction. Had she flinched ever so slightly?

'I'm afraid you'll see mention of Riplingham Barn.'

'In here?' Stanley said innocently, indicating the newspaper.

He was intrigued as to how she would explain it. Whether or not she'd be forthcoming with all the details. Six months wasn't long. Surely it must still be painful.

'It's not the type of publicity that's helpful when you're just starting out. You know, when starting a business. It's the type of thing that might put some people off.'

'From staying at the barn?'

'Yes,' she said. 'Hardly what you want associated with a holiday rental. Death, I mean.'

He wondered whether she'd ask him if he'd changed his mind about staying. Was a refund about to be offered?

To think that it was the complete reverse. The dead man was the very reason he was here. Chances were that she may even know that.

It'd crossed his mind that a touch of notoriety might actually be beneficial for trade. People, he found, have a fascination for the macabre. Too insensitive, perhaps, to suggest at such an early stage. Just something to consider in the future.

'Somebody died here?' Stanley asked.

'Goodness, this isn't the welcome I'd hoped to give

you.'

'It's okay. If you don't want to say.'

Bridget looked around. Stanley wondered at what.

'Well, you'll find out one way or another,' she said. 'Littleworth's like that.'

'A small place.'

'Indeed. News travels fast.' As if deciding to move out of earshot, she said: 'Let's walk up to the barn and I'll tell you about it. You can come back for your car when I've shown you around.'

She led him across the road to the entrance of a laneway beside the cottage. The track was uneven and pitted.

Stanley sensed that she might've been waiting for someone to talk to. An opportunity, perhaps, to unburden herself of the story.

'This place belonged to my brother, George,' she said. At saying his name aloud, Bridget looked to need a moment to compose herself. 'It was him. He was the person who died here.'

Her voice was uncertain. The tone in which she spoke was unclear.

She continued: 'I was always worried about him. Patrick said I worried too much.'

'Worried?' said Stanley. 'Why were you worried about him?'

'Does the name Simeon Dean mean anything to you?'

Stanley had done his research, but he wanted to hear it from her. 'No,' he replied.

'Simeon was an artist. His work was contemporary. Modern stuff that I couldn't really appreciate. George

17

was his husband. Although not, perhaps you might say, in a conventional sense.'

Stanley had read the stories.

'You say Simeon *was* an artist?'

'Their lifestyle in London was chaotic. They lived in a warehouse. Something of a party pad where everything was done to excess.'

'Drugs?'

'You name it. They liked to push boundaries. Lived life fast. Not worrying about the consequences. Unfortunately, Simeon pushed it too far and died of an overdose.'

Stanley was interested in her account. She'd sanitised the account. From what he'd uncovered, the drug in question had been a party one. The incident had involved rent boys. Why had she chosen not to share all the details? Embarrassed? Wary?

'Were you concerned for your brother's welfare?'

'Simeon's death hit George hard. He didn't know how to process it. Their relationship might have looked unusual to outsiders, but they were genuine soul mates. It was as if George didn't really know how to function on his own. They'd been together so long. He became something of a recluse. He locked himself away for a while, before deciding that he needed a clean break from his London life.'

'Did you think the change would do him good?'

'The Sussex countryside has accommodated creative folk over the years, so I could see it might be healthier for him.' Stanley guessed she was referring to the Bloomsbury set.

As if to demonstrate her point, Bridget nodded at the roof of the building over the hedge. 'That's Flint Cottage. It's where Ursula Moor lives.'

'The author?'

'Yes,' Bridget said. 'She lives there with her partner Quentin Ashcroft. An example of the creatives who've made this location home.'

Stanley committed the names to memory. Never could be too sure when this type of information might come in useful.

Bridget returned to her explanation. 'I think George thought he could reinvent himself. Get a bit of distance from some of those unhealthier influences. Try to find a better head space.'

It sounded like a reasonable explanation.

They'd walked to a point where an impressive building appeared before them. Its honey-coloured beams glowed in the sunshine.

Stanley drew to a halt. He'd read enough to know that the view before him was important. 'It's a beautiful spot. Such a tranquil hideaway.'

Bridget wrung her hands. He sensed her mixed emotions. He intended to provoke a reaction from her. The tears that welled up in her eyes looked to be sincere.

'I hoped that being in Littleworth might've helped George escape. Naïve of me, probably. These things have a tendency to follow you, don't they?'

Stanley listened attentively. 'What happened to him?'

'The inquest concluded that he'd been drinking. It was a cold winters night. He'd tripped or stumbled. He must've hit his head in the fall.'

'I'm sorry,' said Stanley.

'It was me who found him lying there face down in the water.' She pointed at the position in the pond.

'A terrible shock.'

Bridget's gaze lingered on the glassy water. Reflections flickered on its surface. For a moment she looked entirely lost in her thoughts. Stanley supposed that she was seeing the scene again in her mind's eye.

'It was a living nightmare,' she said. 'There'd been a snowstorm so the authorities found it difficult to get through. Not that the ambulance would've made a difference. He'd been dead for several hours. Nobody could survive in the cold for that long.'

Her account raised questions in Stanley's mind, but to ask them immediately might raise suspicion. Or possibly not. At this time, he couldn't be certain of anything. Each step forward looked like a move on a chess board. He'd decided to keep his cards close to his chest. The most important thing would be to initially gather an accurate picture of the scene. Then he could fit together the pieces that led up to George's death. Clues might lie anywhere.

'It hardly looks like the same place now in the sunshine. I can't bear to think of him lying there alone for all that time.'

'It sounds very difficult.'

'Yes. We were just numb to begin with. I couldn't help feeling that it was a consequence of other things. Like it was always going to happen.' Stanley wondered what she meant. 'There wasn't a chance to process what had happened. When you hear stories like that on the news, you don't stop to think about the fallout. You don't realise that it's only the beginning. That there will be police investigations, coroners, inquests and reporters.'

Stanley ventured to ask the question at the crux of it all. It was the very question he believed had brought him to Littleworth: 'Do you believe it was an accident?'

'When the powers that be tell you that's what happened, what's the point in wondering otherwise?'

It was a stance that Stanley had once held himself. Until, that is, he'd seen enough examples of the potential risk in trust being placed blindly in authorities or institutions.

Now he preferred to keep an open mind. To consider that life is rarely black or white.

'You're entitled to an opinion,' he said.

'To think that it could've been anything other than a dreadful accident only leads to such terrible places. In the immediate aftermath, with the police interrogating us, it felt as if we were all suspects.' Stanley assumed she referred to a close-knit circle of local residents. From her description of that night, the snowfall had limited those with an opportunity to cause George harm. That's not to say an outsider couldn't be entirely ruled out. It just looked unlikely.

'You could say it upset the apple-cart,' she continued. 'It made us look at one another with suspicion. It didn't bring out the best in all of us.'

Stanley thought again of small places. The melting pots of relationships between those that reside in them.

Places where the anonymity of big cities or towns didn't exist.

She pulled the keys to Riplingham Barn from her pocket. 'We've got to accept the outcome and move on. There's no appetite to keep raking over it. Littleworth needs closure.'

It was hard to say whether she believed that such a devastating event could be papered over. Surely, even returning to the very spot she'd found her dead brother would repeatedly open up the wound? Besides, Stanley knew that his own presence signalled that this was wishful thinking on her behalf. Somebody, and he didn't know who, certainly believed that there was more to this tale. Regardless of what any outcome may have concluded.

They approached the glass door to the barn. The photos online hadn't done it justice. Its interior was contemporary and minimalistic.

'It's much as George left it,' said Bridget as she turned the key in the lock. She gave a brief outline of the facilities in a way that sounded rehearsed. The mention of wi-fi would be useful for his ongoing research. The hot water, she said, ran off a tank of oil. Not uncommon, apparently, for rural properties to be off grid. 'There's a kitchen garden out beyond the pond. Help yourself to any of the things growing there. The Plough, the pub across the road, serves food. The owners haven't had it easy. So many pubs struggle to survive these days.'

She clutched the keys in a moment of reflection. She looked around the barn's interior almost reverentially as if she was trying to muster up the spirit of her deceased brother.

'This place has been a godsend,' she said. 'Every cloud has a silver lining, don't they say?'

'Indeed they do,' said Stanley, thoughtfully. 'Indeed they do.'

CHAPTER THREE

Patrick walked the perimeter of the land to inspect the fencing. He cursed himself for not bringing a notepad and pencil, having instead to create a list in his head of what needed repairing. The list grew ever longer.

He found Jimbo crouching industriously with his tools at a stile. His long hair and beard were reminiscent of a biblical carpenter.

'No wonder this one's seen better days,' said Jimbo. 'There's more foot traffic here than Oxford Street.'

'The ramblers have right of access. They're legally entitled to cross the land.'

'I bet they don't think about who has to maintain everything.'

'A double-edged sword. They might bring litter and damage, but they also bring business.'

Patrick knew that some of the locals spoke disparagingly of the seasonal visitors, but places like The Plough depended on them, and they were a stream of income he too hoped to harness.

Jimbo got to his feet. He ran his hand over the gnarled wood. 'I've done a patch up job for the time being. But it's going to need a bit of attention.'

Patrick added it mentally to his list.

'Isn't it incredible how powerful nature is?' said Jimbo. 'It sleeps in the winter. Then roars back into life when the seasons change.'

Patrick nodded. The efforts to tame the wilderness were constant. Beyond the rural idyll that the ramblers observed, lay the reality of back-breaking hard work and toil.

That's why Jimbo's extra pair of hands had proved to be such a gift.

Patrick watched as Jimbo's nimble fingers rolled a cigarette.

It wasn't unusual for the warmer weather to bring stragglers to the farm. Patrick's childhood summers had been an ever-shifting cast of seasonal players. Back then, many were foreign and spoke very little English.

'Are you comfortable in the van?' asked Patrick. The vehicle was parked not far from the house. They'd run a cable to hook him up to the power.

'It's got everything I need.' Jimbo'd told him that he'd converted it himself.

'There are spare rooms in the house.' Patrick had offered before.

'Thanks. But I like my own space.'

Bridget hadn't leapt at the idea of a stranger in their midst. 'What do you even know about him? He could be an axe murderer. Or on the run.'

Patrick had laughed. He took her point. 'He seems decent enough. Just a bit of a misfit. And, quite frankly, I need the brute strength.'

Bridget wasn't sure. 'You say he'll camp out in his van?'

'Yes. He can access the outside toilet and tap.'

'Doesn't it seem odd that he hasn't got a home? How old is he?'

Patrick hadn't asked. It'd been hard to guess under all that hair. 'I'd say he was in his thirties.'

'Perhaps he hit hard times,' Bridget said, apparently softening her stance.

'Or maybe it's just the way he wants to live.'

'You mean rejecting the material things? Refusing to accept the nine to five rat race?'

'I don't know. Possibly.'

'A non-conformist, perhaps.'

Patrick couldn't offer absolute reassurance. It was a risk. His gut instinct told him that the stranger wouldn't cause them any problems, which had been enough for Bridget to agree.

Jimbo took a drag on his roll-up. He squinted. 'Where do all these paths actually go?'

'Some lead up to the peak of the downs. Others form part of the south downs way. They stretch for miles along the south coast. Linking up towns and villages.'

'They've probably looked the same for years.'

'Maybe just a little more overgrown in places.'

Jimbo scanned the vista. His gaze meandered across the sweep of the land. The slopes of the terrain.

Patrick found him difficult to read. He didn't like to talk about himself. A man of very few words. Ultimately, an amiable presence about the place with an impressive work ethic. Not only mucking in when instructed, but also having the initiative to make suggestions. Turning his hand to whatever needed attention.

'There's work here for as long as you need it,' said Patrick.

Jimbo didn't reply.

Patrick wondered whether there was a reluctance to commit. Maybe it would've gone against the non-conformist principles Bridget and Patrick had speculated he held.

It would be a shame if he moved on. Patrick would be sad to see him go. He'd enjoyed having another man about the farm. It'd almost balanced up the numbers.

In fact, with Jimbo's presence and the conclusion of the inquest, Patrick almost dared to consider that there might be hope. The sunshine held potential. Such a contrast to the bleak despair they'd faced not so long ago.

Jimbo finished his cigarette and gathered up his tool bag. Together, they made their way back across the land in easy small talk. They shared opinions on how the farm could develop in more sustainable ways. Jimbo had a penchant for all things organic. To talk of such things lifted Patrick's spirits. It signified the prospect of new beginnings. The start of looking to the future, instead of always dwelling on the past.

Everything, he thought wrongly, was about to improve.

CHAPTER FOUR

As a person driven by instinct as much as reason, Stanley decided it was time to tell her the truth. He'd not anticipated making such a disclosure so soon. Instead, holding a belief that operating undercover would be best. Yet through this briefest of interactions with her, Stanley understood that to induce any person to speak about events without raising suspicion would be virtually impossible.

'I'd like to be honest with you,' he said.

Bridget, who was in the motion of laying the keys to the barn down on the table, froze. 'What do you mean?'

'I already knew of your brother's death. It's actually the reason I'm here.'

Her hand hovered above the keys as if she might snatch them back and ask him to leave. 'Who are you?'

'I'm a private investigator.'

He tried to judge her reaction. The cogs were turning. To what conclusions she was drawing he couldn't tell. In effect, the pin on the metaphorical grenade had been pulled. No chance to undo it now.

'A private investigator? What does that mean? Do you work for the police?'

'I work for myself. I'm completely independent. Anyone can employ me and my services.' He hoped that by explaining he might build some kind of bridge between them. 'Usually my work involves companies who want assistance in uncovering cases of fraud. Occasionally I assist in cases of infidelity or trying to track down missing persons. In regards to this case, the circumstances are slightly unusual.'

He was glad she appeared more intrigued than angry. 'Unusual? In what way, unusual?'

'In regards to my client.'

'And who might that be?'

'I don't know,' said Stanley. 'That's what's unusual.'

Stanley explained, as best he could. He'd received an anonymous email in response to his standard advert online. The stranger had visited his website. The address they'd emailed from bore no indication of age or gender.

'What did their email say?'

'There wasn't much detail. They sent a link to a news report about your brother's death. The sender stated that they doubted whether George's death was an accident. They believed he'd been killed.'

Bridget wrapped her arms around herself as if suddenly feeling cold. Perhaps the memory of that bitter January morning had returned to her.

'That's not what the inquest concluded,' she said again, and yet this time her words sounded empty, like she didn't really believe them herself.

'I was in two minds about the email,' said Stanley. 'They said they'd send through enough funds for me to book two weeks here at Riplingham Barn and to cover me for two weeks of wages.'

'It was fortunate that the barn wasn't booked.'

'Serendipitous, perhaps?'

She didn't answer.

'I wasn't sure of the ethics. To not know the identity of a client.'

'But the prospect of being paid won you over?' He thought this rich considering the lavish barn that looked to have come into her possession.

'Believe it or not, my motives are well-intentioned. Having read about your brother, I wondered, *What if*? What if a miscarriage of justice had occurred? These things happen. It's not impossible.' He spoke again from personal experience.

Bridget began to pace back and forth. 'I don't like that you let me say all those things without telling me who you were.'

'I've told you now,' said Stanley. 'Would you have spoken differently had you known? There was nothing incriminating in what you said.'

'Is that what you hoped? For me to unwittingly give some kind of confession?' The conversation was in danger of escalating. 'How do you know that this client of yours isn't just somebody wanting to cause trouble?'

He wondered whether she had someone in mind.

'Tell me plainly, Bridget. Has it ever crossed your mind that George's death might not have been an accident?'

'You've asked me that already.'

'I did, and you evaded the question.'

She looked through the glass out towards the pond. Her shoulders slouched as if defeated by the never-ending situation. 'Of course I wondered. From the moment I found him I asked myself whether he'd been the victim of foul play.'

'But you didn't say anything?'

'It wasn't as easy as that. George's character made the incident entirely plausible. The weight of evidence was against me. I think some people saw his demise as inevitable, a lesson to others about the danger of living a different type of life. I sensed that even the police didn't care. As if by him being who he was somehow made him less important. Nothing more than a sorry statistic.'

Stanley recalled what she'd said about being afraid of embarking upon possibilities of wrong doing. He sympathised with her. To feel the weight of opinion against you and to fear the consequences of challenging this was a difficult, and potentially isolating, position to be in. Not to mention vulnerable. For if George had actually been killed, what danger might she be in if she chose to pursue the guilty party?

'I can see it from both sides,' said Stanley. 'I appreciate your desire to move on. You've suffered enough disruption. On the other hand, I believe you loved your brother. If there's even the slightest doubt that his death might not have been an accident, it's going to eat away at you forever. Bit by bit.'

'Are you asking me to help you?'

'I'd like you to think about it. To uncover whether any wrongdoing's occurred, I need to avail myself of all the facts.'

'Aren't they already at your disposal?'

'The broader aspects of the case, yes. But in regards to the finer details, I don't have the evidence the police investigation gathered. I'll need to rely on old fashioned detective skills.'

Bridget looked him in the eye. 'You're going to dig the dirt on all of us. Is that what you're saying?'

'I wouldn't put it like that. Initially, I need to collate an accurate picture of the potential crime scene. To try and establish whether there are any clues as to what exactly happened. After that, the investigation will move on to gathering witness accounts in order to find out who was in the proximity. I'll need to consider whether there was any possible motives to harm your brother. Also, to weigh up who might've had the means and opportunity to commit the crime.'

It was a lot for her to absorb. Stanley wasn't even sure himself whether the mountain ahead could be conquered. The outcome of the inquest didn't bode well for him to prove otherwise.

'I don't know how the residents will react. I doubt they'll respond well to a stranger. They won't appreciate things being raked over again.'

'I'll be as sensitive as I can. I give you my word,' said Stanley. She didn't look reassured. 'I think the chances of gathering a conclusive account of what happened would be greater if you were to help me. People may be more willing to talk if you can discreetly assist me in the background.'

'Undercover, you mean?'

'To begin with, yes.'

He hoped she was coming round to his way thinking. He'd taken a punt that the bond between the siblings had been a strong one. His hunch looked to be correct.

'George wasn't always the easiest of people to get along with. He was often misunderstood.'

'He was a human. Everybody has different sides to them. Light and shade. I promise to look at everything from all angles. I'll do my best to reserve judgement.'

They'd barely moved since entering the barn. He'd said his piece.

It would take trust on her behalf to engage with him. He was prepared to build that rapport with her. His gut said that Bridget was the one who knew George the best. He hoped her insights could get him closer to the man he'd never had the opportunity to meet.

'If only George were here to tell us what happened,' said Bridget, as if she'd read his mind.

'I hope that by hearing what everyone has to say on the matter, George's voice might still be heard.'

Before arriving in Littleworth, it'd crossed Stanley's mind that George's sister might've been his mystery client. A close relative would seem like the obvious individual to want to question his death. Perhaps there might be genuine doubts about how he'd died. Or perhaps it could be a last futile attempt to delay the finality of death.

He wasn't sure now. If she was bluffing, Bridget was a skilful actress. He'd scrutinised her reactions. They appeared convincing.

'I understand if you need to discuss it with anyone

else first. I don't need an immediate decision.'

Stanley thought he'd detected something shift in her demeanour. She stood a little straighter. Something in her eyes spoke of defiance. Not someone who needed to seek permission from others.

'I'm quite capable of making my own decisions,' she said. He liked this display of independence. 'I'll do what I can to help you.'

'Thank you.'

'I reserve the right to change my mind though if I have any doubts about your methods or motives. As I said, I don't know what type of reception you'll receive in Littleworth. You'll have to tread carefully.'

Bridget's tentative willingness to work with him was a significant step forward. Her local knowledge and connections may prove to be invaluable. Stanley felt buoyed by this development. He'd arrived with little more than hope and an open mind. Now, with a first bridge built, potential avenues to explore began to open up before him.

She suggested that perhaps Stanley might like to get settled at the barn before doing anything else. She'd give him a chance to unpack and make himself at home.

They began to walk together back up the laneway so that he could collect his car. On passing the pond again, Stanley ventured an initial probing question: 'On the morning you found him, you say George was lying face down?'

She confirmed this as correct.

Stanley wondered why he'd been facing the pond? It

suggested that if he hadn't tripped maybe he'd been pushed from behind. Unless, of course, his body had been moved.

'What was he wearing?'

'I only really remember that he was wearing his red coat. It looked so out of place against the white of the snow.'

To be wearing a coat suggested that George had been somewhere or was heading out somewhere. Where would he have been going on such a wintry night? There was a chance he could've put on a coat to have a cigarette if he was a smoker.

It was in these details that Stanley hoped to reach a better understanding. A gathering of the facts to find a way – a path, you might say – to the heart of the possible mystery of George Thorpe's death.

CHAPTER FIVE

Having brought his suitcase inside, Stanley contemplated his surroundings.

Despite Bridget's assertion that George's presence could still be felt at Riplingham Barn, Stanley sensed little of the deceased owner. The neutral décor gave the impression of a place that had been wiped clean. Any personal touches had been effectively erased.

Only a striking painting in the lounge looked to be a remnant from the past. Stanley peered at it. A signature in the bottom right-hand corner was that of Simeon Dean. It looked like an original. Stanley, who was no expert in such matters, wondered whether it might be expensive.

So much today could be purchased on credit. It made it difficult to differentiate between those who were truly well off and those whose lives were a façade built on debt. In Stanley's opinion, the root of most crimes lay in either money or love.

Whilst initial research had revealed Simeon Dean to have made significant earnings from his artwork, there was no certainty that the cash hadn't been squandered. The types of excess Bridget had alluded to would not come cheap. Too easy for cash to trickle away. Believing, perhaps, that money would always flow.

Riplingham Barn was the only potential evidence of George's financial situation. It looked like he'd sold their trendy warehouse in London after Simeon's death and purchased his new home in Littleworth. Which, in turn, had come into the possession of his sister. Presumably through instructions in his will.

It was a possible trail. A potential line of inquiry.

Stanley would need to tread carefully.

These thoughts tumbled through his mind as he set out on foot to undertake an initial reconnaissance of the vicinity. Locking the door, he looked again at the ornamental pond. Hard to fathom that's its pretty demeanour belied its recent tragic history.

At the end of the laneway, Stanley came across a figure closing the picket gate at Flint Cottage. A tall man with a slight stoop. He wore a pair of spectacles that gave the impression of academic curiosity. From his sensible clothes and salt and pepper hair, Stanley guessed at him being in his fifties.

'A visitor?' the man said, on seeing Stanley.

'Yes,' said Stanley. 'I'm staying at Riplingham Barn.'

'Another member of the ever-changing cast. We'll have to get used to all these passing faces.'

'I'm Stanley.'

'Quentin,' the man replied beyond the apparent safety of his garden gate. 'My partner is Ursula Moor.'

Stanley remembered Bridget's description of the couple. Creative? Was that the word she'd used?

'The author?'

Quentin looked pleased at the recognition of Ursula's name. Stanley only hoped that he wouldn't be questioned on her books as he hadn't read any.

'The very same!' Quentin said, grasping his fingers together in delight. 'I'd invite you in to introduce you, but she's working in her study. She works in silence. Doesn't like to be interrupted.'

Stanley didn't like to look, but he thought he'd caught a twitch of a curtain in an upstairs window. A surreptitious glance caught the flash of a pale face before it vanished back into the murk.

'An inspiring place for a writer to live, I should think.'

'I look after all her business affairs,' said Quentin, as if this was important. Not always easy, Stanley thought, to live in the shadow of someone creative. It brought George to the forefront of his mind. 'I deal with all the boring stuff, so that Ursula doesn't have to worry about it. It allows her to focus on writing without any distraction.'

How quickly the conversation had turned to Quentin. Stanley wondered whether it might be a sign of insecurity. A need to be recognised, perhaps?

'Have you lived in Littleworth long?'

'Ursula inherited Flint Cotttage from her godmother over twenty years ago. Just when her writing career was beginning to take off.'

'It looks to be completely unspoilt. Littleworth, I mean.'

Quentin's stoop looked to be suddenly more pronounced. The weight of the world looked to be upon his shoulders. 'It's a delicate balancing act. Trying to preserve what makes us unique, but also having to adapt to new ideas in order to evolve and survive.'

It sounded like he'd given it some thought.

'New ideas?'

'Everyone brings with them suggestions as to how Littleworth can adopt new ways. We seem to have had so many new faces in the last few years.'

There was something in his voice that suggested that this period of change might have been unsettling. Stanley wondered to which new faces Quentin was referring. George, undoubtedly, would be one of them. Hadn't Bridget said too that she and her family had been relative newcomers?

'I suppose what happened in January must've been difficult too?'

Quentin squinted. 'You heard about that?'

'It was in the newspaper. I asked Bridget about it.'

'Yes, I suppose it's common knowledge now. Unfortunate that we should be associated with a story like that. Rather a dark cloud to hang over such a beautiful place.'

It was a cold assessment of the situation.

'It looks unspoilt,' said Stanley again.

Quentin's reticence suggested otherwise. Such things ripple unseen beneath the surface. Maybe undetectable to the innocent eye of a passing visitor.

'It attracts all sorts. Some are drawn by the natural beauty of the downs. Others, I think, are fascinated by its history of artistic folk.' Stanley thought again of the bohemian Bloomsbury set. A group of writers and artists who had found solace in the Sussex countryside and one another's company. 'A modern type of folklore, I suppose.'

It occurred to Stanley that George's death might become a part of this narrative.

Sensing that Quentin might be an eager oracle of local myths and legends, Stanley seized the moment: 'You must've come to know the man who died?'

Quentin nodded solemnly. 'His name was George Thorpe. You'll have seen that in the newspaper. He moved down here from London.'

'Quite a different way of life from the capital, I should think.'

'Exactly. That's very perceptive of you. The pace of life in the country is slower. That's what makes it special.'

Stanley murmured gentle noises of agreement in the hope that Quentin might continue to share more information.

'I found him rather abrasive, to be honest,' said Quentin. 'Not really fair to speak ill of the dead. There was just a lack of respect. No appreciation for tradition and the way things have been done around here.'

Was there a whiff of entitlement in Quentin's words? Was this a man used to calling the shots? Before Stanley had the chance to weigh this up, Quentin continued:

'He seemed like an impatient man. A consequence maybe, as you say, of fast city living. Quick to offer his opinion on how things might be done differently.'

'Like what?'

Quentin looked towards the farm and then The

Plough. 'Oh, George liked to have his say on everything.'

It was a vague unsatisfactory answer.

'So you kept George at a distance?'

Quentin gave a dismissive laugh. 'Not so easy to do that in a hamlet like this. Not when the person concerned is an immediate neighbour. What's the saying about keeping your friends close but your enemies closer? Ursula felt that we should give him the benefit of the doubt.'

'She wanted to give him a chance?'

'You could say that. It's in Ursula's nature to take care of things. Always the first to champion an underdog or take in a stray kitten or wounded animal. There's usually somebody or something she's ready to take under her wing.' Stanley wondered whether this difference of opinion between them had caused any friction. 'Ursula believes in keeping the peace.'

It was difficult to gather information by stealth. The conversation skirted around things leaving an impression of things unsaid. Stanley was being deliberately cautious. Better to be seen as an overly inquisitive tourist rather than someone with a vested interest. In this vein of nosey neighbour, he continued with his gentle line of questioning.

'Had you seen George on the day he died?'

'Yes,' said Quentin. 'There was a gathering in The Plough that evening to celebrate Imogen's birthday. Imogen is the daughter of Bridget and Patrick from Downlands Farm.' Quentin's eyes glassed over as he summoned up the memory of that evening in his mind's eye. 'Ursula insisted that we should attend. Not only for Imogen, of who she is fond, but also for the sake of the local pub. Important to give them our business. But I digress.'

'And George attended?'

'Yes. Imogen was very fond of her uncle. She was very close to him.'

'So the pub was busy?'

'No, not at all. You see, a heavy snowstorm had set in that day, cutting Littleworth off entirely from the outside world. It was a peculiarly small affair. I'm not sure Imogen wanted a party at all. Besides her parents and uncle, and me and Ursula, the only other people present were Will and Zara.'

'Will and Zara?'

'Landlord and landlady of The Plough. Nice couple. Trying to make a go of it in the face of economic adversity. Somewhat of an uphill struggle.'

Stanley felt pleased that a picture of that evening was emerging. It was only one viewpoint, but it was a broadening of the perspective. George's whereabouts prior to his body being discovered in the pond somehow brought him slightly back to life. It marked the beginning of re-tracing his footsteps.

'You must have been shocked to hear about his death?'

'Not really. To be frank, it didn't surprise us at all. If you'd seen the state of him that evening, you wouldn't have been surprised either.'

'He was worse for wear?'

'Some people become mellow or soppy when they

drink. Whereas others become volatile and unpredictable. George, evidently, was the latter. He was wound up like a coiled spring. He seemed to be on edge. Ursula thought he was insecure about feeling like an outsider. She said he wanted to be *liked*.'

'But you didn't agree?'

'I think there was something bitter about him. That evening he seemed to me to be seething with unspoken resentment. He wanted to show off. To be centre of attention. Some people are like that, aren't they? Prone to histrionics and hoping to shock.'

It was beginning to feel as if Quentin held some type of prejudice against George. Stanley wondered whether he'd disapproved of George's lifestyle.

'So George walked home alone?'

'Walked? Staggered, more like.'

'Nobody thought to check he got in okay?'

It was the closest Stanley had got to passing judgement. Quentin clutched the picket fence.

'All well and good looking at these things with hindsight,' he said. 'If you'd been there, you'd have seen that George had rather burnt his bridges. I don't think there had been a lot of goodwill left for him.'

Quentin's blunt overview of the situation sat at odds with the newspaper account in which tributes had been paid. It raised as many questions as it did answers.

'Not much point dwelling on the past now,' said Quentin, briskly. 'About time we all put the nasty business behind us and moved on.'

Again, based on his words and demeanour, it looked

unlikely that Quentin was the identity of Stanley's mystery client. Based on this briefest of encounters, Stanley couldn't say that he'd witnessed the creativity Bridget had referred to. The word that sprung to mind was more *traditionalist*. The type of man who wasn't adept at change. Preferring the comfortable parameters of the known in favour of the uncertain risks of the new.

In bidding each other farewell, Stanley felt an aloofness from the man. Someone more concerned with looking inwards than out at his surroundings. A tragedy in such a beautiful place.

With his head whirring with possibilities and ideas, Stanley set off in the direction of the solid looking building across the road. He needed to see with his own eyes the location of George's final evening alive…

CHAPTER SIX

Will Solomon sometimes found it hard to remember the dream they'd had. Looking back, they'd been incredibly naïve. To think that he and his wife, with no previous experience, could turn around the fortunes of a failing country pub where others had dismally come undone.

He remembered the day they'd first visited. Dismissing the boarded-up windows and overgrown beer garden and instead convincing each other of the untapped potential. They'd bounced ideas off one another about the prospect of developing it into an upmarket gastropub with rooms to rent. Maybe even with a microbrewery attached.

Zara, with a passion for design, was already re-configuring the layout in her imagination and transforming the various spaces of the old inn.

The Plough embodied the opportunity they'd been seeking to reinvent themselves, with the seclusion of Littleworth offering the privacy they craved. Not having worked in the hospitality trade, they hadn't grasped the enormity of the venture. Or the public face that such a business required.

Just the knockdown price they'd bought the place for should've sounded alarm bells. But instead, it had only convinced them that destiny was on their side. As if, perhaps, The Plough had always meant to be theirs.

It depressed Will to think that many of the issues they'd hoped to escape from their old life had simply been replaced with different ones. Foolish, he thought now, to believe that reinvention might ever truly be possible. They'd underestimated the baggage carried with them from the past, and woefully misjudged the energy and determination needed to keep a business like The Plough afloat.

The whole enterprise was a juggling act. Everything from paperwork, finances, orders, cleaning, staffing.

Having looked fretfully at the takings in the till from the lunchtime trade, Will leant against a beer pump on the bar and contemplated his domain. It oozed historical charm and character. Gnarled wooden beams, flagstone flooring and leadlight windows. A fruit machine flashed in the corner. A couple of tourists sat beside the unlit fire in the inglenook fireplace, making their pitiful soft drinks last as long as they could. The TV screen on the wall had a rugby match playing. The whistle blew for half-time, and Will watched nostalgically as the players huddled together in comfortable camaraderie.

At that moment, the door to the public bar opened.

The fellow who entered looked suave. He wore chinos and a navy blue shirt with sleeves rolled up deliberately to his elbows. Not your typical south downs straggler, Will thought. A man, perhaps, of intellect.

The man's owlish eyes blinked, adjusting from the glare outside to the perpetual gloom of the wood panelled interior. He looked studiously around, apparently determined to take in every tiny detail.

'Hello,' said Will in the role of jovial landlord.

'Good afternoon,' replied the man as he approached, wherein he lay his seemingly manicured strong hands upon the smooth wood of the bar. He spoke in a languid and drole way. 'Such history in these old pubs. If only the walls could speak.'

'Let's be grateful they can't,' Will laughed.

The man pulled up a bar stool and perched upon it. He sat upright and alert. 'May I have a pint of local bitter, please?'

'How about a Sussex Bedlam Ale?'

'If that's what you recommend.'

Will breathed in the tangy aroma of hops as he pulled a frothy pint of amber gold. 'What brings you to these parts?'

'I'm staying at a holiday rental across the way.'

'Riplingham Barn?'

The man nodded. 'My name's Stanley.'

'Nice to meet you, Stanley,' said Will as he placed the drink on a brass drip-tray. 'I'm Will.'

'Ah, the landlord.'

'You heard?'

'I just ran into a neighbour of the barn. He told me that you run this place with your wife.'

'Yes,' said Will. 'Let me guess, was it Quentin Ashcroft? Font of all local knowledge.'

47

Stanley lifted his glass and gave a nod. He sipped the ale reverentially, looking determined to savour each exquisite flavour within the drink. He nodded again in approval and swiftly licked the bubbles from his top lip.

'He filled me in on some of Littleworth's history,' said Stanley.

'I bet he did. Or more like he took an opportunity to gossip.'

'Not a fan of his?'

'He's more of an old woman than that writer he lives with.'

The tourists by the inglenook were starting to move, gathering up their coats and rucksacks. Will often wondered how many tales had been spun in that very spot. It was the kind of nook where countless Quentin Ashcrofts must've sat and peddled gossip over the years.

'Quentin told me how important it was to support you with their custom.'

Will threw back his head and laughed. 'A few half pints of shandy and the occasional bag of peanuts is hardly going to keep the wolf from the door. That's typical of him to be portraying himself as a saviour. Sanctimonious old git.'

Stanley's face remained impassive.

Will gave a wave to the tourists as they exited.

'What else did he tell you about Littleworth?' he asked. 'I expect he was keen to share all the morbid details of Riplingham Barn.'

'To be fair on him, it was me who asked the

questions.'

'You did?'

'There was a report in the newspaper about the inquest into George Thorpe's death. I was intrigued.'

'I suppose you would be, staying at the barn.'

'He told me there'd been a gathering here on the evening before George's body was discovered. To celebrate Imogen Heywood's birthday.'

'Yes. Imogen sometimes works behind the bar here. She's on a gap year. Has a pleasant manner about her. The customers like her.'

'Quentin said that she wasn't really keen on a party.'

'She's actually quite shy. I don't think she likes being the centre of attention.'

'Quite the opposite of her uncle then?'

'Is that what Quentin said?'

'He described him as outgoing. Attention seeking? Flamboyant, even?'

'That doesn't sound like a very flattering description. Not a particularly kind way to speak of the dead, eh? But then, I don't think the two of them saw eye to eye. Sort of like chalk and cheese.'

Will scrutinised the man's face for any signs of what he might be thinking, but his expression remained resolutely unchanged.

'What didn't they agree on?' asked Stanley.

'I don't really know. I got the impression that George appreciated the beauty of Littleworth and thought it should be shared with others. I think he saw it as a place of recovery that could be beneficial. He wanted Riplingham Barn to be a sanctuary.'

'He wanted to throw open his doors to visitors?'

'That was his plan. Not a particularly well-developed plan. But a plan nevertheless.'

'And Quentin didn't like the idea?'

'Quentin and George were very different people. Perhaps Quentin feared being outnumbered on his own turf?'

'Or maybe a nimby?'

'Quite possibly. In his defence, I suppose he felt a bit surrounded at Flint Cottage what with George living on one side and the Heywoods on the other.'

Stanley sipped his ale. 'It sounds like George and Quentin clashed.'

'I suppose so.'

'Yet Quentin said that his partner took George under her wing?'

'Ursula? Yes, that's right. I think she considered him a fellow creative soul. They tend to gravitate to one another, don't they?'

'Strength in numbers I should think,' observed Stanley. 'Feeling a together-ness at being mutual outsiders?'

'Sounds feasible. Although Zara reckoned Ursula was just looking for material for her latest book. She said we'd probably all find ourselves in one of her novels eventually.'

Stanley broke a smile. 'I wonder if it caused any conflict between the two of them - Quentin and Ursula, I mean?'

Will shrugged. Speculating publicly on other people's relationships when working in the pub trade required caution. Far too easy to be identified as the source of an unflattering story. Or run the risk of attention being turned on one's own marriage; so searingly public in their line of work. 'Who knows what goes on behind closed doors,' he said, dismissively.

'Quentin said that George had burnt his bridges with everyone. What do you think he meant by that?'

'There are ways of going about things. Especially in small communities like this one. I think it takes time to get people onside, for them to trust you.'

Stanley reflected his words back at him: 'And did *you* trust him?'

'To have Littleworth's best interests at heart?'

'Yes.'

What had only been six months suddenly felt like a vast chasm. That was the thing with time, Will had discovered. It had a habit of playing tricks on you. Slowing down and speeding up when you least expected it. Sometimes being invisible, and sometimes rearing out unexpectedly like a jack in the box.

'I don't know what George's intentions were. That evening, it was like he'd got trapped in a maze. Not a real one, you see. But one in his head.'

'Quentin said he was on edge that evening. Wound up like a coiled spring.'

'Well, that's something I'd probably agree with Quentin on. He was like a bomb waiting to explode.'

'Do you know why that might've been?'

Will had more than strong views on the subject, but replied: 'No. I don't.'

'From a stranger's perspective, it looks like a terrible tragedy. A man trying to overcome his own grief. Trying to turn things around in a new place. And yet maybe I see things through rose tinted glasses. Not fully grasping all the aspects of the situation.'

'Nobody deserves to die that way,' said Will.

The conversation appeared to have reached a dead end. Will noticed that on the TV the second half of the match was about to kick off and turned his attention to it.

'You follow the rugby?' Stanley asked.

'It's a bit of a passion. Once it's in the blood and all that. We can be a bit fanatical.'

'Have you ever played?'

'Yes. I played professionally for a time.'

Stanley looked to be impressed which pleased Will immensely, then made him feel inexhaustibly empty. Those sporting days could've been yesterday. Although, of course, they weren't.

They watched the game re-commence. Will sensed that Stanley's engagement with the match was purely superficial. Before long, the visitor's eyes began to roam about the place. His inquisitive gaze looked to ponder the position of each table and chair, and each door. It was as if the man were sketching a mental floorplan. Committing every last detail to memory.

'I shall have to come back when you're serving food.'

'You'd be welcome,' said Will, thinking again of the meagre takings in the till.

'I might get to meet your wife too?'

'I'm sure Zara would be happy to meet you.'

Stanley got to his feet. He'd left the dregs of his ale at the bottom of his smeary pint glass. 'Thank you for your hospitality. It's been a pleasure.'

'Likewise,' said Will. 'I hope you enjoy your stay in Littleworth.'

The landlord watched as Stanley sidled away as smoothly as he'd arrived. The door closed behind him.

Will hadn't bought a word of it. It wasn't the first time they'd experienced it. Previously they hadn't seen the signs.

But they'd learnt.

Much more alert to these things now.

In the past, they themselves had been the outsiders.

He didn't believe for moment that a man with so many questions was only staying for a vacation. No, this Stanley - if indeed that was even his name - had the hallmarks of someone on a mission. Once again, Will had the sinking feeling that the ghosts of the past were threatening to return from the dead to haunt him.

CHAPTER SEVEN

(i)

To: stanley_messina@PIservices.co.uk
From: TJ1989@datamail.com

RE: Investigation into death of George Thorpe

Dear Mr Messina,

Just a quick courtesy acknowledgement of your arrival at Littleworth. I trust that the funds transferred to your bank account were sufficient to cover the cost of hiring Riplingham Barn and to cover the initial agreed fee for your services.

Again, whilst my anonymity may seem irregular to you, I hope that in time that you'll appreciate my need for discretion. I don't want to prejudice you in the course of your investigation.

Sincerely,
Your Client

Once Stanley had neatly unpacked his meagre belongings, he took some time to reflect upon the information he'd gathered so far regarding the potential case surrounding George Thorpe. Stanley, himself being unphased by spending time in his own company, wondered whether George had been of similar character? Whilst some people are comfortable alone with their thoughts, others require constant stimulation and the company of others. From what Stanley had deduced so far about George's relationship with Simeon Dean and the buzzing lifestyle they'd had in London, it followed that George would've fallen into this sociable category.

It brought to mind the phrase about the devil making work for idle hands.

Had George, Stanley wondered, had too much free time on his hands following his move to rural Sussex? Had Simeon's death left him at a loose end? From Bridget's brief description it had sounded as if the pair had been very close. So perhaps the loss had left George rudderless? Looking for the type of new direction that Will had hinted at.

Stanley sat on the leather sofa. He looked up at the abstract painting by Simeon Dean.

The barn struck him once again as soulless. Its minimalism wrought the place devoid of any emotion. Thinking again that perhaps it represented a slate being wiped clean.

A sense of what had gone before the discovery of

George's body was beginning to emerge. The Plough had accommodated a small circle of people to mark Imogen Heywood's nineteenth birthday. Those in attendance had been Imogen and her parents Bridget and Patrick. Also, landlord and landlady of The Plough, Will and Zara Solomon. Then there had been Quentin Ashcroft and his partner Ursula Moor. And, of course, George Thorpe himself.

A heavy snowstorm had cut Littleworth off from the outside world, therefore limiting the number of people who could have had the opportunity to cause George harm.

From accounts so far, George had been inebriated and, for reasons unknown, he'd seemed on edge or erratic. The initial opinions given also hinted at possible underlying tensions stretching back further than events of just that evening. As yet, these tensions weren't specific. Just vague suggestions of mild disagreements between local folk.

There didn't appear to be any hidden method as to how George had been killed. If he hadn't tripped, as the inquest had concluded, it seemed most likely that a decisive shove from behind had caused his death. No particular skill required for such a means of killing. Although, perhaps, it pointed at something spontaneous rather than anything meticulously planned?

Either way, any of the people at The Plough that evening could've been capable of pushing a drunk man into an icy pond. All of them, as far as Stanley could see, had the physical means to commit the crime.

Bridget's description of discovering George's body hadn't highlighted any peculiarities. Only the wearing of his coat had pointed at George being deliberately outside - maybe never having made it inside when returning from the pub. It occurred to Stanley too that the continuing snowfall that night would've covered any possible footprints.

It was easy to see how the inquest had drawn its conclusion. There was a narrative suggesting that George was prone to substance abuse. A narrative only compounded by the death of his partner who had actually died of an overdose. If, and it was still very much an *if*, George had been deliberately killed, the perpetrator had been lucky. Very much a case of being in the right place at the right time. Or, in George's case, the wrong place at the wrong time?

With no further handle on who his mystery client might be, Stanley still had serious doubts. What if George's death really had been nothing more than a tragic accident? Was he being led up the garden path? And if so, how far would he go before considering the damage that might be done to his own reputation?

Stanley didn't sleep well that night. To lay his head where George had once laid his, felt uncomfortable. A new experience to be in the very place under investigation. Living and breathing it.

Unorthodox, to say the least.

His night was interrupted by the seemingly disconnected names and faces he'd encountered. Perhaps subconsciously his brain was scurrying to put the random pieces together. Trying to connect the dots.

He got up early the next morning and stood beneath the shower in the stark bathroom. As the water cascaded down on him, a plan as to how best to move forward began to form in his mind. It would do no good to have this myriad of ideas floating about. Extremely unsatisfactory. He chastised himself for failing to remember his own mantra of distinguishing between facts and opinions. Both would be important in trying to understand the psychology of Littleworth and its residents. Opinions might not be one hundred percent reliable, but they often paved paths towards the truth.

Just a matter of then deciding which of these to follow.

Stanley patted himself dry with one of the expensive fluffy white towels provided. At the moment, it felt like only blind alleys. Just initially picking up a metaphorical torch and shining it into the dark corners. Hoping to reveal hidden details that might prove once and for all whether George's death had been an accident or not.

Stanley dressed.

Determined to build an even more accurate picture of the backstory, he placed his trusty espresso maker on the polished gas range and drew up a stool to the vast kitchen island. As the aroma of coffee wafted around him, he opened his leather-bound notebook and wrote down the names of those who'd been at The Plough that evening. His handwriting was tidy and elegant.

On the next page, in large letters, he wrote 'MOTIVES?'.

It might be awkward, but he would need to confirm with Bridget that Riplingham Barn and George's belongings had come into her possession following his death. If so, there was a chance she'd benefitted significantly. Her husband too.

Had the Heywood's faced financial difficulties? Hadn't Bridget said something about the barn being a 'godsend'? It was something to ask more questions about.

Continuing along this train of thought, Stanley wondered what had brought Bridget, Patrick and Imogen to Littleworth in the first place? He made a note of this on another page on which he'd written 'RESEARCH'.

Bridget and her brother had sounded close to one another. But was there anyone else in their family? And what had Bridget *really* thought of Simeon Dean?

Next, Stanley turned his attention to the neighbours at Flint Cottage.

From all accounts, Quentin and George had not seen eye to eye on things. Will Solomon had suggested that George had intended to 'open up' the barn to visitors. It raised questions as to whether simmering tensions between the two could've boiled over into open aggression? A flimsy motive for killing someone. But, Stanley knew, stranger things have happened.

Too soon to rule anything out.

And what of Quentin's partner, Ursula? What were the exact details of her link with George Thorpe? Had she just wanted to help him, as Quentin had said? Or was theirs a genuine friendship?

Stanley couldn't discount that there might even be more to it. But that would be pure conjecture. No concrete evidence to support it. Just another question to write in his notebook.

That just left Will and Zara to contemplate.

As with the Heywoods, Stanley wondered what had first brought the Solomons to Littleworth. Yes, he knew it was The Plough. But what had prompted them to buy a remote pub in the middle of nowhere?

There didn't appear to be any obvious connections between George and the owners of The Plough. And thus, no obvious motive. It didn't mean that there might not be hidden links. The only certainty - the only *fact* - was that it had been the location of the most likely suspects that evening. This alone deemed it necessary to consider Will and his wife with suspicion.

Stanley poured himself a thick black espresso.

There was much to think about.

Opportunities. Means. Motives.

Also, lingering in the midst of it all, potentially hidden in clear sight, was the mystery identity of his client. Somebody with their own motive to delve into all these uncertainties. Somebody, perhaps, pulling strings? With good intentions? Or bad?

Stanley sipped his drink. He looked again at the painting on the wall. The artwork was ethereal. Something other-worldly about it. Random or deliberate strokes of Simeon Dean's paint brush?

Much like this case, Stanley thought. Random or

deliberate.

The way ahead didn't look straightforward. That, Stanley thought, was most definitely another fact.

Despite not having at his disposal the luxury of the significant resources available to the police, a couple of hours of online research proved decidedly fruitful for Stanley. The information he sought wasn't classified or restricted, but instead freely and readily available.

Earlier in his career, Stanley had had qualms about this aspect of his new profession. He'd always valued and respected privacy in his own life. So, in effect, to spend any amount of time snooping into the lives of others hadn't sat easily with him. Over time, however, he'd come to appreciate that information in the public domain was fair game. So much of people's lives - especially in an increasingly technological world - was documented online. By gathering these nuggets of information, backstories could be fleshed out to provide valuable insights into the histories and potential motivations of the individuals under investigation. To not get fixated on the final destination, but instead to re-trace the steps that had led to it was Stanley's philosophy. All lines of inquiry to be laid out like lines on a road map.

The pages of his notebook, which earlier that day had been blank, were filling up fast. He had learnt a great deal. It was bringing life and nuance to that initial cold list of suspects. Providing an opportunity to contrast what he'd now learnt with what might've been portrayed to him in person. Giving hope that these juxtapositions might lead him closer to a definitive outcome in the case of George Thorpe.

The key, as any historian would attest to, was to establish the reliability of each source. To consider fully the intentions behind them.

In Stanley's opinion, it was best to treat them all with caution. Never jump to wild conclusions. Things aren't always as they seem, regardless of the apparent authority in which they've been conveyed.

Stanley imposed a strict policy upon himself to always handle the information gathered with sensitivity and respect. Because whilst so much could be found by legitimate means, he believed it important not to use any information as unnecessary collateral against an individual. Not to diminish anyone, unless absolutely necessary.

The aim was to uncover more tracks. To discover things that would help navigate a way through the woods.

What he'd discovered online was certainly enlightening.

Amazing what additional information could do to present complete strangers in an entirely different light.

It made him wonder whether he might've viewed Littleworth another way had he known. And it raised the awkward question as to whether the residents too were entirely aware of each other's histories and reputations.

Only time would tell.

CHAPTER EIGHT

To ground himself again in the locale, which after some time at his laptop screen had morphed into somewhere foreign and obscure, Stanley decided to stretch his legs.

He trudged back up the laneway. George again played heavily on his mind.

It was quiet. The stillness only broken by various birdsong which, not being an expert on ornithology, Stanley couldn't attribute to any particular breeds.

Back at the top of the laneway, he took a moment to survey the panorama again. The view, one that probably hadn't changed for decades or longer, encompassed the homes of all those names listed in his book: The Plough, Downlands Farms, Flint Cottage.

His brain buzzed with thoughts.

During the morning's research, he'd allowed himself to speculate on the types of motives in other cases. With no obvious reasons for anybody wanting George dead, Stanley wondered if mulling over potential motives might offer a speculative way into the case. Jealousy, perhaps? What if someone had been jealous of George? That was the type of thing that might drive a killer. What might they've been jealous of? Or what if George had posed a threat to someone? In what way? Stanley wondered whether there was potential to damage anybody's reputation. Which brought to mind vanity. That, of course, couldn't rule out the possibility of blackmail. But there'd been no evidence of that so far.

Light clouds scudded gently above the horizon. There was the very faintest of breezes.

Again, Stanley was struck at how Littleworth's tranquility belied the events of its recent past. A scar upon its perfection. Maybe undetectable to the unknowing eye, and yet there if you chose to see it.

Had he imagined it, or had he seen again a twitch of a curtain at an upstairs window at Flint Cottage?

Just then, his attention was drawn to a person's movements in the middle distance.

He hadn't noticed them until now.

On a raised triangular mound of grass stood an old-fashioned telephone box. A relic from the days before mobile phones. Its red paint and small panes of glass looked at odds with its rural surroundings.

Following a hunch, Stanley set off towards it.

A young woman with long black hair emerged from its confines, dressed in floaty tie-dyed garments.

On seeing Stanley approach, she gave a wan smile and held the door ajar for him.

'Are you wanting to look in here?' she asked.

The question puzzled him. How should he respond?

Only as he got closer was he able to see inside and comprehend. Like so many things at Littleworth, the telephone box was not what it appeared to be. It was something else entirely.

'A library?' said Stanley. 'I would never have known.'

She opened the door wider to give Stanley a better look at the inside of the box which had been expertly decked out with shelves. On each of these were colourful rows of books.

'We don't call it a library,' she said. 'It's more of a book exchange.'

'A wonderful idea.'

'Thank you. It was me who thought of it.'

Stanley had an inkling who this young woman might be, but she was first to establish identities.

'Are you staying at the barn?'

'Yes. I'm Stanley.'

'Ah, so you've met my Mum. She would've given you the key.'

'You're Bridget's daughter.'

'Yes. I'm Imogen. The barn belonged to my Uncle George.'

'Your Mum explained.'

'Did she?' she said quietly.

Her reaction was pensive. It might not be advisable to bombard her with intrusive questions at this moment. A danger that she might withdraw from him entirely. Not the time to go at things like a bull at a gate. Better, perhaps, to try and build a bridge. Focus on establishing some kind of rapport.

'What gave you the idea for a book exchange?'

She lowered her head as if embarrassed or shy. She said coyly: 'Books are my passion. I've always loved reading.'

'A fellow bookworm,' he said.

His response seemed to embolden her. 'Ah, so you enjoy books too?'

'Indeed,' he said.

'Lots of people say that nobody reads books these days. Too attached to their phones. Not enough time. Or short attention spans. As if reading is a luxury rather than a necessity.'

'You want to show otherwise?'

Imogen leant against the open door of the telephone box. 'They decommissioned this box and were threatening to take it away. I knew that lots of visitors pass by. Some people were not sure about the idea. They thought it might attract unwanted attention or be vandalised.'

'But you persisted?'

'George encouraged me to pursue the idea. He thought it was the type of thing that Littleworth needed. New life. New ideas.'

'Well, it looks to have been a success.'

'Yes,' said Imogen. 'Even old Quentin from Flint Cottage came round to the idea eventually. Especially when he saw some of Ursula's titles on the shelves.'

'Are you only interested in reading? Or would you like to be a writer yourself?'

Her eyes looked up again shyly at him through her black lashes. 'I've always wanted to be a writer. For as long as I can remember it's what I've wanted to do. Even from an early age. Way before we moved to Littleworth.'

This last statement sounded important. Her tone of voice suggested that it held some kind of significance to her.

'I should imagine being a writer isn't easy,' said Stanley.

'That's what everybody says. When I was at school, I got told that writing isn't a proper career. They said that it isn't a job and that nobody ever makes any money from it. Well, not enough to live on anyway.'

'That must have been discouraging.'

'Not really,' said Imogen. 'In fact, it made me more determined. It's made me want to prove everybody wrong. I just kept my ambitions to myself.' She glanced in the direction of the books on the shelves. 'This is part of my way of showing that it's possible. If Ursula Moor can do it…'

Her voice seemed to drift away.

'You were lucky to move somewhere that had an author in residence,' said Stanley.

'Lucky? Yes, I suppose so.'

'Have you had an opportunity to ask Ursula about her writing? I imagine she'd be able to share with you some of the secrets of her success.'

Imogen twisted the toe of her shoe on the grass beneath her. Stanley sensed a reluctance to look in the direction of Flint Cottage.

'Yes, I've spoken a little bit to her about it.'

It was a cool response to his question.

Perhaps the question had shown ignorance on his behalf? Whilst not identifying as a creative individual himself, he had maybe overlooked the unique processes that such artists pursue. Disrespectful of him to paint everyone with the same broad brush. Creative types could often be mysterious. Rightfully protective of their approaches and methods. Had Imogen encountered any of this resistance from the local author? They were certainly both from different generations.

'Bridget said that you haven't lived here very long? It must've been a wrench moving out to the countryside?'

'Not really,' said Imogen. 'I was at a crossroads in my life anyway. I'd just finished my studies at college so things were going to change anyway. It wasn't as if I was going to see my friends every day after that.'

'Why did your parents choose to move to Littleworth?'

'My grandparents lived at Downlands Farm. When my grandfather died suddenly, my parents realised that my grandmother Joyce, wouldn't be able to cope with the farm alone. It's a lot of hard work.'

'Yes, I can imagine,' said Stanley. 'And your parents were interested in agriculture?'

'I'm not sure how much what *they* wanted really came into it. It all happened so fast.' She closed the door of the telephone box. 'Aren't parents usually an enigma to their children? Isn't that the normal way of things?'

Stanley guessed she would make an excellent writer. She was astute and articulate. He would have to see whether he could find anything she had written.

'So do you think you'll stay here?'

'Oh no,' said Imogen. 'This isn't a place for young

people. It's where you get washed up in the future. When things haven't worked out how you'd planned.'

It was a damning assessment, but based on the information he'd uncovered, entirely understandable why she might hold such an opinion. A little harshly expressed, however. Especially bearing in mind what had happened to George.

Washed up?

She began to walk away in the direction of the farm. Her dress caught on the breeze. Her hair roiled.

She turned but kept on moving away, taking backward steps. 'George said we're all just stories in the end,' she said, cryptically.

Then she spun on her heels and headed back towards the farmhouse. A solitary figure against the sweep of fields.

CHAPTER NINE

On his return to the barn, Stanley was surprised to see someone through the archway to the walled kitchen garden. Slightly concealed by foliage, their movement was enough to catch his eye.

The person unknown suddenly brought home to Stanley exactly how privately the barn sat within its boundaries. Would anyone hear if he were to call out? Only, he supposed, the residents of Flint Cottage might be close enough. Even then, the walls looked thick.

With George again playing heavily on his mind, Stanley tentatively advanced in their direction. He moved beyond the pond, and then passed on his left-hand side the monstrous green tank that housed the oil for the barn's hot water and heating. An oppressive silence descended upon the scene. The absence of birdsong gave a sense of menace that Stanley hadn't felt so far at Littleworth.

'Hello?' he said.

A cloud moved in front of the sun. The tumbling foliage of overgrown vegetation within the hidden garden lost their colour in the shade. No longer lush and green.

'Hello?' he said again. 'Anybody there?'

A slow scrambling noise, like that of an animal, arose as a woman raised herself into view. She groaned at the exertion of getting to her feet.

'Hello?' she echoed, looking around absently to identify who'd spoken.

Was there a hint of fear in her eyes? Did she harbour any of the same concerns about being alone and vulnerable in this place with its troubled history?

'Over here,' said Stanley with an accompanying friendly wave and smile, which on seeing her face softened and lit up into an impish smile.

'Are you Stanley?'

'Yes.'

'I'm Ursula. You met my partner, Quentin.' She brushed her skirt down with her gloved hands. 'I didn't hear you. I was quite away with the fairies.'

'I wasn't creeping up on you.'

His words fell flat. The smile upon her face seemed to freeze momentarily as if she was somehow stuck in time. Then, she twitched back into life.

'I'm not trespassing,' she said. 'Don't want you thinking I'm snaffling. There's always been a tradition here, you see. Sort of a communal arrangement. Everyone who lives in Littleworth can chip in to look after the garden. With the understanding that in return they can help themselves to what is grown here.'

She eyed the proliferation of weeds and much of the crops that had gone to seed.

'It's not looking its best,' she continued. 'I'm not sure how much time the others are putting into it. The responsibility seems to have fallen on me.'

The concept of community gardening was not a new one to Stanley. It reminded him of childhood holidays to distant relatives in Italy. However, the open access aspect of the garden in light of his investigation didn't sit comfortably with him here.

Ursula spoke again: 'I think it's been more neglected than in previous years. That's probably no surprise, all things considered. I expect people are wary of coming down that laneway alone. Quentin said you'd heard what happened.'

'Yes,' said Stanley.

'People can be superstitious about these types of things, can't they?'

'It hasn't worried you? You haven't felt unsafe?'

She shrugged. 'They said it was an accident. What are the chances of lightning hitting the same spot twice?'

'It would be very unlucky.'

'The garden's become a little wild. I quite like that. It's good to come and get my hands dirty after hours of writing. Brings me back to the real world. Grounds me, you might say.'

Stanley stepped forward and saw that a trug at her feet brimmed with fruit and vegetables. The garden, whilst unkempt, was clearly productive.

'I was only just speaking with Imogen about her aspirations of being a writer,' he said.

Ursula wiped her brow. 'Such a lovely young girl. So full of life and energy. We need more like her in Littleworth.'

Where had Stanley heard something similar said

before?

'It hit her terribly hard, of course,' said Ursula. 'She'd really only just got to know her uncle properly. They'd become close. Death to young people can come as such a shock, don't you think? It can shatter their sense of immortality. Utterly shake their foundations.'

In recalling his conversation with Imogen, Stanley wasn't sure he'd witnessed any particular distress. Time had passed, of course, and what shows on the surface isn't always congruent with what lies beneath. Even so, his impression of her had been one of resolve and resilience.

'I shouldn't want to be a young person again,' said Ursula absently as if talking about something else entirely. 'Trying to work out who you are. Thinking about what you want to be. All those decisions and choices.'

'Have you given Imogen any advice?'

'Oh, I have a rule *never* to tell anyone what to do. I just encouraged her to listen to herself. Not to get caught up with what other people think. Other people's opinions can be so loud.'

Stanley wasn't sure he'd got the full picture, but he followed the gist of what she said.

'So many problems begin in childhood,' she went on, seeming determined to press home the point she wanted to make. 'I fear that might've been true of George and his sister. From the snippets he shared with me, I don't think their early years were easy.'

'No?'

'They were brought up by their grandmother. I don't

know all the details. Reading between the lines I think things were difficult. A suggestion that perhaps their mother was some kind of addict. These things can run in families, can't they?'

Stanley wasn't so sure. But perhaps this tale might be worth storing in the memory bank. Something to gently ask Bridget more about to see if it had any bearing on the bigger picture.

'Quentin said that you got on well with George. You became friends?'

Ursula tilted her head. There was something bird-like about her. She looked inquisitively at Stanley as if she might be considering him as a potential character in a future book.

'I was pleased to see somebody creative,' she said. 'This area of Sussex has a tradition of welcoming writers and artists.'

'Ah, the Bloomsbury set.'

'Among others, yes. Are you artistic, Stanley?'

'I would call myself an appreciator. Sadly, I wasn't blessed with a creative talent.'

'I don't believe it's a matter of being born creative or not. George and I agreed on that. We tended to see eye to eye. Perhaps not always on the way he went about things, but in the general sweep of ideas we had a similar outlook. He, like me, believed that these things can be learnt. He felt it was important to share knowledge and experience. To help others harness their creative imagination.'

It was probably the most sympathetic description of George Thorpe he'd encountered so far.

'I'm not sure how imaginative I am,' said Stanley.

'You appear to stand very straight, Stanley. Yet there's an inquisitive twinkle in your eye. Which suggests to me you have strong powers of observation, and in my experience, observation and creativity go very much hand in hand.' The impish smile returned to her lips. 'You've certainly gleaned a lot of information about us here in a short space of time, I understand.'

Stanley wondered what Quentin had told her about their conversation. Maybe his presence in Littleworth was arousing suspicion?

'I can't deny I've been curious,' he said. 'It does sound like an unusual situation. An intriguing set of circumstances?'

'It was an accident. That's what the inquest concluded.'

'So I keep being told.'

'Do you have reason to believe otherwise? What have people been saying?'

Stanley thought he noted a tone of passive aggression in her voice that hadn't been present before. Was she protective of Littleworth's reputation too? Could she be protecting the man she'd befriended? Or was there something else behind her defensiveness?

'Not everyone has spoken as warmly of George as you.' Stanley recalled Quentin's opinion but thought better of provoking her with it. 'I sense that he wasn't afraid of making waves. Stepping on other people's toes, perhaps.' It was all supposition, but he hoped to garner her perspective from it.

'I understand that he was acting somewhat erratically that evening,' Stanley continued.

'Erratically? That's subjective. Sometimes it's the fool who is ignored that is the only one brave enough to speak the truth.'

Stanley guessed it was a Shakespearean reference.

'Besides,' she said, 'to link his behaviour that evening to his death suggests that the two might be connected. An example of cause and effect, perhaps? Which suggests you are more creative than you say.'

Stanley felt the conversation was floundering, but decided he might as well plough on. 'I'm interested in what *you* think. I understand you were at the gathering at the pub that evening.'

'Yes,' she said. 'And I was one of the first to learn of his death the following morning.'

'You were?'

'I was in the front garden. It was early. I was still in my dressing gown. The snow had fallen so heavily, I wanted to admire the scene. It was like Littleworth had been transformed into another place; somewhere magical.' She paused, but Stanley didn't interrupt her train of thought. He waited patiently for her to carry on. 'I was lost in my own thoughts. My mind was on other things. I didn't notice Bridget approaching until she reached our fence. I remember thinking how lucky George was to have a sister nearby to look out for him. I think I even commented on it to her.'

'And after that?'

'Bridget walked away down the laneway to the barn, and I went back inside. But within minutes she'd

76

returned and was knocking fiercely on our front door. She said she thought George was dead. She couldn't get reception on her mobile phone, so asked to use our landline. It's all a bit of a blur. I couldn't really believe what was happening. I remember shaking uncontrollably and Quentin trying to calm me down. He always thought George was trouble.'

Stanley noticed how tightly she gripped the handle of her trug.

'So Bridget rang the police? An ambulance?'

'Yes, she must have. As I say, it's all a bit blurry. I had a lot on my mind. The issue, of course, was that the snow prevented them from getting through. Bridget asked us to go back with her to where she'd found George.'

'Did you?'

'I did. I was worried for Bridget. She was in such a state. I didn't think she should be alone. I suppose there was part of me that wanted to see for myself, as I couldn't really believe it.'

'And Quentin?'

'I'm not sure he really believed what had happened. I suspect he thought George was just play-acting. Making a scene. Quentin can be a bit funny about that type of thing. So I didn't push it with him. I was thinking on my feet really. I put a coat on over my dressing gown and walked back with Bridget to where she'd found him.' Her gaze moved in the direction of the pond, visible through the archway to the garden. 'There was no doubt that he was dead. Bridget was distraught. She was saying things like, "Do you think it matters that I've touched him? Have we disturbed the scene?" So I just tried to calm her down. She wanted to kneel by him and hold him, but it was freezing. Eventually we moved inside the barn and looked through the window at him lying there. It was all very unreal. We were sort of stuck in time until the authorities arrived.'

She looked haunted by the events.

'It feels like both a long time ago and, yet, as if it has only just happened. Isn't it funny how time can do that?'

Her spirit appeared to be returning.

'You didn't answer my question,' said Stanley. 'As to whether you thought there was a connection between George's death and events that happened prior to it?'

'I'm a writer, Stanley. I let my imagination run away with me sometimes. I have to. Of course I've wondered whether there was more to George's death. But this isn't a *story*. This is real life. Sometimes in life, accidents *do* happen.' It was true. Stanley had experienced this first hand. 'I'm just sad that some of George's ideas will never be realised now.'

She stared, with a vacant melancholy expression, towards the furthest corner of the garden which looked to open up on to an overgrown patch beyond. Stanley felt as if he was intruding upon her quiet reverie. What was she looking at?

Then, as swiftly as she'd drifted away, her attention returned and she was shuffling on her bird-like feet through the garden towards him.

'Here,' she said, rummaging in her trug, 'you must

have some of this lettuce. Just look at the size of these radishes!'

CHAPTER TEN

Just as she'd done on the morning she'd discovered George's body, Bridget wrung out the dish cloth and grabbed a tea towel to dry the breakfast dishes stacked in the drainer.

The kitchen cabinets were old-fashioned and some of the doors hung askew on their ancient hinges. It would benefit from a re-vamp, and they had the funds to do it now. But how to negotiate such change in the face of such stiff opposition would require a reserve of energy that Bridget didn't know whether she held. She wasn't heartless. She'd always been sympathetic, considerate of her mother-in-law's feelings. It was just that it didn't always feel like *their* home.

As if on cue, the clump of heels on sensible shoes approached from the hallway.

Bridget turned wearily. Sometimes it felt as if they lived with a ghost.

'You look pre-occupied,' said Joyce.

In the past, Bridget had thought of her as an immovable force. Totally unashamed of being outspoken and voicing her opinions. Although even Bridget had to concede that since the loss of her husband, Joyce had softened at the edges. Almost finding common ground in their own particular griefs.

'I was thinking about George,' Bridget replied.

'I think about Doug. It's a way of keeping them alive. Just a little bit.'

'It's just…'

'What?'

'It's that evening before he died,' said Bridget. 'I keep turning it over in my mind. I wonder if there was something that I missed. And whether there was something, *anything,* I could've done to change what happened.'

Joyce looked uncharacteristically anxious. 'It'll do you no good to dwell too much on it. We have to try and look forward.'

Easy to say, but Bridget doubted whether Joyce was following her own advice. This farmhouse, this *museum*, was practically a shrine to Doug. It embodied an unspoken clash between past and present.

Just then, Bridget saw through the window the reason for her unsettled state of mind striding purposefully towards the farmhouse. The private investigator, Stanley Messina.

She hadn't mentioned his profession, nor the conversation they'd had, to anybody else.

'Who's that?' said Joyce. 'Do you know him?'

'He's the latest guest at the barn. His name's Stanley.'

'Staying there all alone?'

'Yes,' said Bridget.

Joyce made a grunt that sounded like disapproval. It was why they tried to keep her away from the visitors.

'I wonder what he wants?' she said.

Bridget cast the tea towel, and the interaction with her mother-in-law, aside and dashed out to intercept him.

On seeing her, he raised his hand in a confident greeting. He struck her as the type of person one could trust. Their paths met, causing them to stop face to face.

'Is everything okay?' she said, panting slightly from her dart from the kitchen.

He looked kindly at her. 'It's the water at the barn,' he said. 'I can't seem to get it to run hot.'

'Oh,' said Bridget. 'That'll be the oil. The water temperature can be temperamental when it's running low. I think it's due for a re-fill soon. I would have to ask Patrick. He deals with those types of things. I'm very sorry.'

'No need to apologise. It's not the end of the world, and you did say I should drop by if there was any concern.'

'Yes,' said Bridget. 'Yes, absolutely.'

She glanced back towards the kitchen window but the sunlight on it disguised whether they were being observed.

'I also wondered whether you'd had a chance to think any more about what we discussed? I was hoping to ask you a few questions.'

'I've thought about it a lot. You planted a seed of doubt.'

'I did?'

'Yes,' she said. 'It's got me turning over everything

again, churning it all up, asking myself questions. Had I missed something? Was there anything I didn't know about?'

Bridget suddenly felt exposed out in the open. Patrick and Jimbo might return from the fields at any moment, and anyone might be looking from the farmhouse.

She said, in a lowered voice, 'I haven't told anyone else. You know, why you're here.'

'Are you free to talk now? Am I interrupting you?'

'Let's talk. But not here. Come this way.'

She led him up the winding path that skirted the old house. Beyond the yard and where Jimbo had parked his camper van, stood the summer house they'd bought for Bridget to use as an office. A purchase they'd been able to afford due to the proceeds of George's death.

'I insisted on keeping the business side of everything separate from family life. I didn't want it in the home. Too many lines to be crossed.'

'Very sensible,' said Stanley.

It made her consider where the lines lay for him. Did he have an office somewhere? How did he balance life and work? Before she had the chance to ask, he was already speaking: 'It can't have been easy moving into what was, to all intent and purposes, somebody else's home?'

'You go into these things with good intentions, don't you? I think we all wanted it to work, but we hadn't thought through the practicalities.' She opened the door to the summer house and looked proudly at the order and neatness. It was furnished with simple yet functional furniture: a desk, a filing cabinet, a couple of comfortable chairs. A noticeboard screwed to the wall displayed a planner with future bookings for the barn clearly marked.

'It looks like you enjoy having a tidy mind too,' Stanley observed.

That had been her reputation. One that she'd built her entire career upon.

Until, of course…

'When we moved here, I floundered. I wasn't sure what my role should be. It was hard to define myself in an environment that belonged to Patrick's parents. There was so much history to contend with. Only in time did we grasp the enormity of a small holding and start to allocate responsibilities. Please, take a seat.'

'You said Patrick's father died? That's why you moved here?'

'Yes. Doug. In the pandemic.' She decided to skip quickly over this topic. 'We knew, Patrick and I, that Joyce wouldn't be able to look after this place alone.'

'You wanted to move here?'

'I don't think we were the only ones to consider a move to the countryside after the lockdowns.'

'Indeed,' said Stanley. 'A big move, nevertheless.'

It wasn't the whole story.

She saw Stanley notice the framed photo of George on her desk.

'Had you always been close to George?' he asked.

'You might say we didn't have a conventional childhood,' said Bridget. 'We never knew our father, and our mother struggled with her mental health and addictions. So we grew up mainly with our grandmother, our mother's mother. I always tried to protect George, being my little brother and all that. I think it all had more of an impact on him than me. Maybe because he was younger.'

It was a very quick account of their upbringing. Condensed into a few brief sentences.

'Did George get on with his grandmother?'

'It was complex. George always tested those close to him. He pushed people to the limit to see whether they might abandon him, like our mother had done. Our grandmother was a kind woman, but she was firm about the rules in her own home. It caused them to butt heads, especially when George became a teenager. Always getting into some sort of trouble. Our paths sort of diverged during those years. There was always a bond between us, but it became rather distant.'

Bridget saw that Stanley listened intently. She couldn't see how any of this could help him in his investigation. Unless, of course, he believed somehow that a potential miscarriage of justice may lie in George's *inherent* character. If it were so, she felt obliged - as so many times before - to leap to his defence.

'George wasn't always an easy person to like. He refused to compromise on what he believed in and had come to be staunchly true to himself. Whether others liked it or not. I think George and Simeon had that in common. They found confidence and strength in one another.'

'Did you like Simeon Dean?'

Bridget saw no reason to be anything less than entirely honest. 'Simeon was fifteen years older than George. I was suspicious of him at first. The age gap didn't sit comfortably with me. Over time I came to see that as my own prejudice. They were actually very well matched in their outlook. I can't say I entirely understood their relationship, but it seemed to work for them.'

'Are you suggesting they had an open relationship?'

'I didn't ask George too many questions. It wasn't the type of thing we talked about. It was clear for anyone to see that they were secure enough between them to explore encounters with other men. Maybe there was a thrill in it? Or perhaps they felt life was too short to be confined to just one person. As I said, they were resolute non-conformists.'

Bridget felt a pleasant sense of unburdening. She didn't know why. It just felt good to talk and, for once, be heard.

'As I said,' she continued, 'we found ourselves on very different paths. I concentrated on my studies and career, then met Patrick and juggled work life with having a baby. Whilst George pursued a hedonistic whirlwind on the success of Simeon's artwork.'

'Did George hold on to Simeon's coat tails?'

'That's what people have said, but I don't think that's fair. I'm not sure that Simeon would have had the success without George. They were definitely a team. One couldn't really exist without the other.'

'As if George was his muse?'

Bridget laughed. 'That's the type of description George would've loved. Though I doubt it was as simple as that. When George turned his attention upon you it could be blinding. He was exciting to be around. He could be incredibly funny. He was a *dreamer*. And the world needs more of them, don't you think?'

Stanley nodded in agreement. 'You speak affectionately of him.'

'I think people are often protective of the dead.' Bridget thought of more than one example. 'I mean, it's not as if they can defend themselves, can they?'

'No,' said Stanley. 'Are you saying George was protective of Simeon after his death?'

'He wanted to create some kind of legacy. I think it was a way of immortalising him.'

Stanley scratched his temple. 'A legacy?'

'He wanted to tap into the narrative of artistic folk who've resided in the south downs. To align Simeon with them. Put him in the same ilk. He never said it explicitly, but I thought that's what had drawn him down to Littleworth. That, and a realisation that the type of life him and Simeon had lived in London wasn't healthy. He needed to remove himself from the bad influences and temptations.'

'How would he create such a narrative?'

'Through storytelling. He'd become fascinated with fables and tales. He believed there was power in telling stories. Like a type of therapy.'

'That's why he wanted to open up the barn to outside visitors?'

'Not the barn, as such. He had the idea of storytelling

87

huts. A bit like those old shepherd's huts. A safe space where creative people could escape to and share their ideas and experiences.'

'Storytelling huts,' said Stanley. 'I like the sound of that.'

Bridget felt a pang of sadness for all the things that would not be now. She wanted to believe that George's spirit still hung about the place. If only she could talk to him just one more time. He had never judged.

'Do you really think there might be a reason behind George's death?' she asked. 'I mean, something from his past? From his life in London, perhaps?'

'I don't know,' said Stanley. 'The past can cast long shadows.'

'But there were only locals here that night?'

'Just as George believed, maybe the answer lies in getting people to share their stories.'

Was it time to tell him her story? She wasn't sure. Besides, it was likely that he already knew. A one-sided version at least.

'It feels like a cobweb being spun. And…'

She paused.

'Yes?' said Stanley.

'It's just I can't help fearing that if we keep on digging, there's a chance that the possible danger might return.'

They looked at one another. Each contemplating the severity of what she'd just said.

It was then that a shriek sounded from the farmhouse.

CHAPTER ELEVEN

(i)

EASTBOURNE TEACHER CONVICTED OF POSSESSING COCAINE BANNED FROM CLASSROOM FOR 10 YEARS

A highly-regarded Eastbourne teacher's career is in ruins after she was convicted of possessing cocaine.

Bridget Helen Heywood has been banned from the classroom for 10 years after the Education Secretary overturned a disciplinary panel recommendation that she should face no professional punishment.

Mrs Heywood, aged 36, claimed that she had picked up the cocaine from a restaurant toilet whilst drunk and had not used the drug.

She says she is openly anti-drugs and resigned from The Lottbridge Academy to spare the school embarrassment following her conviction.

Heywood was convicted at the Lewes Magistrates Court of the offence of possessing cocaine. She was fined £100, and ordered to pay £85 costs and a £20 victim surcharge.

'Don't make a fuss,' Stanley heard the woman say as they entered the kitchen. 'It's just a scratch.'

'There's a lot of blood,' said Imogen, who crouched beside her. A wooden chair lay next to them on its side.

The woman who had fallen, Stanley guessed, must be Bridget's mother-in-law.

'What's happened here?' asked Bridget.

'I was upstairs in my room,' Imogen replied. 'I heard a scream.'

Stanley noticed how pale the girl's face was. Her black locks draped forlornly over her shoulders. She held her grandmother's arm gently, raising it up slowly for everyone to see the wound and blood.

'It's nothing. It looks worse than it is.'

'What were you trying to do?'

'I wanted to make some scones.'

'Scones?' said Bridget, crouching down beside her.

'Yes. But I couldn't find where any of my baking items were. The bowl and sieve weren't where they used to be. *Nothing's* where it used to be.'

It was more of an accusation than an observation.

'You should've asked me where they were,' Bridget said. 'I could've shown you.'

'It's not a good idea to go climbing on chairs,' Imogen added.

'There was nobody around to ask.' Her eyes glanced briefly in Stanley's direction, and despite her vulnerable position on the floor, her pupils blazed with a palpable strength of character. 'I lost my footing. I couldn't reach the top shelf in the cupboard. A ridiculous place to have put them. I nicked my arm on the edge of the worktop when I fell. That's all.'

She was gathering herself up, trying to shake off the well-meaning grasps at her elbow, but reluctantly having to accept the assistance.

Stanley righted the fallen chair so that Bridget and Imogen could manoeuvre her on to it.

'This is Stanley,' said Bridget by way of explanation. 'Stanley, this is Joyce.'

Stanley saw that Joyce's hands were shaking.

'Do you think it will need stitches?' Bridget said, peering squeamishly at the blood.

Joyce's skin looked thin and papery. It was almost translucent, showing the trail of veins running beneath.

'I think it's just a surface wound,' said Stanley.

'Exactly,' Joyce replied.

Bridget, who looked unconvinced, filled a bowl with water and began dabbing away the excess blood to reveal an angry looking graze. Joyce winced as Bridget applied pressure.

'Nothing's where it used to be,' she said again. This time her words were directed at Stanley. He felt that she was hoping for moral support, as if her opinion would be more powerful if a stranger agreed with them. 'Everything has been moved.'

Was that a silent look exchanged between Bridget and Imogen? Had Stanley seen an eye roll?

'No real damage done by the looks of things,' said Stanley. 'No broken bones.'

'A lot of fuss about nothing,' she said, dismissively. Then asked: 'What brings you to Downlands Farm this morning, Stanley?'

He told her about the difficulties he'd had in trying to run hot water. She understood. It was Patrick, she said, who he'd need to speak to about those types of things. He was the one who would be able to fix that for him.

'I'll ask him,' said Stanley.

'You do that,' she replied as if her daughter-in-law and granddaughter weren't in the room at all.

Stanley detected an undercurrent of tension between the three women. 'I ought to get going.'

'You're off?' asked Bridget. 'We can't make you a tea or coffee?'

Joyce squinted suspiciously at Bridget. 'No scones to offer you though.'

'We can make scones,' Bridget sighed. 'If that's what you'd like.'

Stanley politely declined the invitation. 'I'll look out for Patrick on my way back.'

'You'll probably see him in the fields. If not, I'll mention the oil when he gets back.'

'Thank you,' said Stanley.

As he emerged from the gloomy farmhouse, Stanley felt frustrated. It wasn't unusual in cases to encounter a muddle of information. But assessing this case so far was proving to be particularly challenging.

What was it about this isolated hamlet and its people? It was like a closed circle.

The truth, Stanley believed, lay somewhere in the

things left unspoken.

He thought again of the information he'd discovered online. The newspaper report of Bridget's conviction sprang especially to mind. Could it be a coincidence that these events had happened prior to their move to Littleworth? Were they in some way linked? In Stanley's experience, possible coincidences should be treated with caution.

The problem with newspaper stories was their lack of context. Too many blanks to be filled in.

It was all *very* unsatisfactory.

Why hadn't Bridget mentioned her previous occupation as a teacher? During their conversation in her office, he'd provided ample opportunity for her to open up. Perhaps she carried some shame or embarrassment about what had happened. Or maybe she did not yet trust him enough to share her story. Either way, it was likely that she suspected he already knew, with the information being freely available in the public domain.

Sometimes, Stanley knew, fighting prejudice could feel like a pointless task. If others had already painted you with a certain brush, what use would it be to try and paint another picture?

All roads led back to George Thorpe. This whole business of trying to establish whether his death had been accidental or not. It was entirely disorientating, like scrambling around in the dark. Looking at individual things and wondering whether any might be connected in some way.

Whilst theories were beginning to form in Stanley's

mind, he was wary of setting off in the wrong direction. Crucial, he reminded himself, to remain steadfastly open-minded.

He meandered away from the shadow of the farmhouse. It couldn't have been easy moving in with one another, he thought again. All of them under the same roof, such strong personalities. Let alone all having been from different generations. Each with their different viewpoints and ways of doing things.

Stanley had picked up on the unease, barely hidden beneath the surface.

He wondered if they were watching him through the window. Eyes were everywhere here.

Just then, his attention was drawn to a vehicle parked not far from the farmhouse. A campervan. He hadn't noticed it before as its mud splattered and grimy exterior had given the impression of being disused or abandoned. A side door, however, was now open and a figure stood, looking out, from within.

The sun was in Stanley's eyes, so his sight was obscured.

He tried to look closer.

The man had an unkempt air about him. He had scruffy hair and a thick beard. Impossible at a distance to determine how old he might be.

'Hello!' Stanley ventured. His voice sounded small in the open air.

But the stranger flicked a cigarette end out onto the ground before withdrawing back into the van, closing the door behind him without a word.

Odd, thought Stanley.

He might've considered approaching the van if it had not been for the appearance of an old Land Rover, spluttering up the hill towards him. He stepped back as it crunched to a halt on the gravel.

'Stanley?' said the driver through his open window as he unclipped his seatbelt.

'Yes.'

'I thought you might be. I'm Patrick. Bridget's husband.'

Stanley wondered what description Bridget had given for him to be identified so easily. His dapper appearance, he supposed, rather set him apart from the regular day-trippers.

Patrick got out of the Land Rover. He was dressed in jeans, a checked shirt and boots. He reached out and gave Stanley a firm handshake.

'Everything alright at the barn? Settled in okay?'

Stanley relayed again his woes with the lukewarm water.

'It's the oil,' said Patrick. 'That's an oversight on my behalf, sorry. We should've had it refilled in the spring, but what with the place being empty for so long, I thought we could get away with delaying the delivery.'

Mention of the empty barn brought the shadow of George's death over them. It was never far away. Something always being tip-toed around.

'Bridget told me a little of your story.'

'She did?'

'About your move to Littleworth after your father's death. I'm sorry. It can't have been an easy time for you.'

'It was more difficult for Bridget than me.' Stanley thought of the teaching career that lay in tatters behind her and wondered again how this fitted in. 'It was a wrench.'

'You didn't find it a challenge?'

'I'm not saying that. It's just I'd grown up here. I knew what life would be like. If truth be told, I think I got an easier ride from my mother.'

'Joyce,' said Stanley, thinking of the blood.

'Yes. You've met her?'

Stanley nodded.

'Then you'll know that she's a force to be reckoned with. Although, she's really a pussy cat underneath the bulldog exterior.'

'Did she give Bridget a hard time when you all moved in together?'

'I think she was just seeing where the land lay. Trying to work out what the rules of the game were going to be. Inevitable in such a situation, wouldn't you say?'

'I suppose so,' said Stanley.

'I've always been rather let off the hook though. Being the only son and all that. Blue-eyed boy, I guess you might say. In my mother's opinion, I've never been able to do any wrong.'

Patrick hitched up his jeans and placed his hands on his waist. He cast his gaze across his domain. 'Isn't there a saying about not understanding a journey until you can look back at it from reaching your destination? It wasn't an easy time, but I think we were always meant to end up here, for some reason. Almost like it was mapped out for us.'

Stanley knew Patrick spoke metaphorically, but took the moment to look again at the terrain of Downlands Farm. He peered at the green slopes and hedgerows. In the distance, he saw the shapes of tourists moving across the landscape.

'You get a lot of walkers?' asked Stanley.

'Yes. Ramblers. The paths lead across the fields to other villages and towns. They had all become very overgrown. Things had become too much for my old man to look after. Gradually we're restoring things. Important to balance new ideas with preserving things.'

Stanley agreed.

'There are some paths completely hidden at the moment.' Patrick pointed down to what looked like a small area of trees and shrubs. 'That's where the land borders that of Riplingham Barn. It runs behind Flint Cottage.'

The geography of the place began to make sense. Stanley thought of the walled kitchen garden. He had now seen it from another perspective.

'You intend to re-open that path too?'

Something in Patrick's demeanour suggested yet again something unspoken. A world-weary expression fell upon his face for an instant. It was gone as soon as it had appeared.

'That probably depends on how long Jimbo decides to stay.'

'Jimbo?'

Patrick looked in the direction of where Stanley had

seen the bearded fellow in the campervan.

'He's my extra pair of hands. Not easy to find reliable or trustworthy people. The work's tough and doesn't appeal to most.'

Despite the questions Stanley wanted to ask, it was evident that Patrick wanted to get on.

'I'll pop down and look at the oil presently. There's an immersion heater I can show you in the meantime…'

Having bid each other goodbye, Stanley returned again to the theories formulating in his brain.

CHAPTER TWELVE

(i)

The downfall of retail tycoon Hector Lyons had been well documented at the time on rolling TV news coverage, and in both the tabloids and broadsheets. Stanley hadn't been alone in following the lurid details as they emerged, with the public seeming to have an insatiable appetite for every twist and turn in the story.

Having come from humble beginnings, Hector had demonstrated from an early age a passion and drive for entrepreneurship and business. On leaving school with no qualifications, he opened a small hardware and DIY shop in East London, which quickly expanded to a chain of stores across the capital. His real success, however, came in developing the brand into a national franchise of expanded warehouses.

His rags to riches tale proved popular with the media. A capitalist fairy tale for anyone wanting to believe that anything was possible if one put one's mind to it. A fairy tale that Hector himself was more than happy to peddle dressed in outlandish tailored suits and his trademark colourful bowties.

He found himself a darling on the talk show circuit with a natural flair for spinning yarns and entertaining with his stories. Politicians too saw his appeal and courted him ferociously.

His personal life was also colourful. Having divorced two wives in quick succession, his third wife died giving birth to Hector's only child: a daughter. He didn't marry again, and there was intense fascination with the young girl who was the apple of his eye. Hector, happy for her to grow up in the media spotlight, openly spoke of grooming her to be the heir to his empire and fortune.

The fairy tale, as now well-known, was a façade. Behind the glossy depiction of wealth and glamour, lay a growing mountain of debt. Hector, never having shied away from excess, became obese and his health faltered. Having spread his business ventures too thin, he secretly began to embezzle funds from the company pension fund to prop up his crippling empire. He became paranoid and fitted secret listening devices in the offices of his employees and advisers.

An unexpected downturn in the economy saw the business placed in administration, and just as the spotlight began to move towards Hector's crooked dealings behind the scenes, he was found dead on his luxury yacht in the Mediterranean. The official line being that he'd suffered a heart attack. And then, as long serving employees discovered that their pensions had been snaffled, rumours of suicide or foul play arose and refused to go away.

An ugly and protracted court case involving his now

grown-up daughter rumbled on for months, with the prosecution arguing that she had known of the fraudulent activities of the company. Ultimately, she was cleared of all charges. Hector, it was ruled, had even hidden the true extent of the business failure from his absolute nearest and dearest.

This was what Stanley was remembering as he pushed open the door to The Plough. He was trying to recall all the finer details. Hadn't Hector even named his yacht after her?

He looked up and saw her name above the door. Zara. Yes, of course.

Now she was Zara Solomon, landlady of The Plough. But once she had been Zara Lyons – daughter of Hector.

Inside, the pub had attracted a smattering of lunch time trade. Hardly the hustle and bustle Stanley suspected might be required to keep such an establishment afloat. Times were still tough, he supposed. With the price of everything going up, people had tightened their belts. Habits too had changed. The days of regulars propping up bars looked to be a thing of the past.

Stanley walked through the saloon section of the bar to a smaller room laid out neatly as a designated food service area, with neatly arranged tables of which only a couple were occupied. He took a seat at one in the furthest corner of the room in the hope of discreetly observing his surroundings.

A swing door to the adjacent kitchen opened slowly. It was being pushed open by the backside of a woman dressed in a shapeless summer dress and a pair of comfortable running shoes. Her hair was jet black as if it had been dyed and was cut just above her shoulders. She emerged to reveal that she carried a container of cutlery, and that she was heavily pregnant. She moved slowly to one of the nearby tables where she put down the container, then placed a hand in the crook of her back and stretched her belly out before her. Stanley thought he heard her give a small groan.

She pulled back a chair at the table. It looked as if she were about to roll the cutlery into napkins. Then she noticed Stanley's presence in the corner and gave him a little nod before coming over to him.

'I didn't see you sitting there,' she said. 'You'll have to excuse the slower service. Nothing's happening fast at the moment.' She cradled her bump with both hands.

'You look like you're doing well.'

'In my condition, do you mean?' she laughed. 'Being pregnant, I've discovered, doesn't stop you from doing things. It just slows you down.'

'When are you due?'

'Not long now. I'm over thirty weeks. Should probably be winding things back a bit. Not easy being on my feet for so long, but it's difficult to find staff.'

Difficult to bring a baby up in a pub, Stanley thought.

He was scrolling mentally back through the calendar. How many weeks pregnant had Zara been at the time of George's death? Had she even known back then?

Her fringe fell long upon her face. Had he not known, he might not have recognised her at all. She looked

102

nothing like the waif-like blonde he'd seen on the news. Only a trained eye would spot her once familiar face now. No name badge was worn to identify her.

'Are you Zara?' he asked.

She froze. 'Yes. Have we met?'

'No,' said Stanley. 'I've met your husband. I'm staying across the way, at Riplingham Barn. He said I should sample your hospitality.'

Her stance appeared to soften slightly. 'On holiday?'

'Yes,' Stanley lied. 'Will said you haven't been here long yourselves?'

'Not so long, that's right. We moved down from London. I expect Will told you about his injury?'

'No, he didn't.'

She looked surprised. 'That's unusual. He bores most of the customers with the details. He often gets recognised from his professional rugby playing days. He likes to tell them about how he'd still be at it if it hadn't been for his accident. He was crossing a road and got knocked down by a delivery driver on a moped.'

'Was he hurt badly?'

'Oh yes,' she said. 'Doctors said he was lucky to even walk again. Not that Will saw it that way, of course.'

'No?'

'Rugby was his life. To be forced to give it up and seek a new direction wasn't easy for him.'

'But you were happy to leave London?'

She looked tight-lipped. He wondered whether she kept her guard up out of habit. For whilst the scandal of her father lay many years in the past, such things never really go away. There was probably still a curiosity about Hector's daddy's girl. A dwindling market for tittle-tattle stories, perhaps. But a market none the less.

'Littleworth had an appeal. It's got its own charm, hasn't it?'

Stanley wondered whether its potential anonymity and isolation was what had attracted her. 'It's a pleasant place for a getaway.'

'You're comfortable at the barn?'

'Yes. It's got all I need. They've thought of everything.'

'Hard for them to hush up what happened over there though,' said Zara, 'what with the outcome of the inquest and everything. Journalists are such vultures, aren't they? Picking over the remains.' He guessed she spoke not only of George's death.

'It sounds like it was a terrible accident.'

'It does, doesn't it.'

'You don't believe it?'

'Will says I read too many conspiracy theories online. He says that sometimes things are just what they are. He's very trusting.'

'And you?'

'I don't believe everything I'm told. Appearances, in my experience, are often deceiving. Probably got a suspicious mind.'

In light of her upbringing and the alleged dysfunctional relationship with her father, it was unsurprising. How could she trust anyone after such betrayal? Unless, of course, she was thinking of

Hector's death, and the uncertainties that had surrounded it.

'If his death wasn't an accident,' said Stanley, referring to George rather than Hector, 'what reason do you think there could've been for him being killed?'

'Usually close to home these sorts of things,' she said. 'I'd be looking at the family first. They all live together up at Downlands Farm. George hadn't been in their lives a great deal for a long time. Perhaps his rekindled relationship with his sister upset the applecart. You never know how these things can impact upon marriages. Maybe Patrick was jealous.'

Stanley listened.

'George wasn't a saint. We all knew that. Perhaps they were concerned that he might be a bad influence on Imogen, his niece. Parents can be protective, can't they?'

Stanley thought again of Hector.

Zara continued: 'Then, I suppose, you'd have to look at George's immediate neighbours. From what we made out, he became friendly with Ursula – she's the writer. But I don't think he saw eye to eye with Quentin. George wasn't what you'd call Quentin's cup of tea. He didn't want George bringing any other riff-raff to Littleworth. He's pretty small-minded when it comes to things like that.'

'It sounds like you've given it a lot of thought.'

'Well wouldn't you if it all happened on your doorstep?'

Stanley nodded. 'Yes, I suppose I would.'

Then she said, in a hushed voice, 'That just leaves us.

Me and Will. What motive might we have for killing George Thorpe?'

Her making light of the situation didn't sit comfortably with Stanley. The flippant way she spoke suggested a cynical brittle streak within her, as if the untimely death of a man was nothing more than a parlour game.

'You tell me.' said Stanley. 'What reason *might* you have?'

'Nothing obvious springs to mind.'

'You liked George?'

'Yes,' she replied. 'We both did. He brought something different to Littleworth. That's important in a place, don't you think?'

'Indeed.'

Zara suddenly gave a small yelp. 'It kicked! Did you see that? It kicked!'

'A rugby player like its father perhaps?'

Zara didn't reply but ran her fingers protectively over her belly. She gazed down with maternal pride. 'We had tried so long for a baby,' she said. 'We didn't think it would ever happen. It's almost like a miracle. But that's enough of all that. There's a menu on the table and all our specials are written on the blackboard.'

'Thank you.'

'All the produce is sourced locally. We buy as much as we can from Downlands Farm. That's the way of thing in small villages. We have to stick together. Prop each other up.'

It was a virtuous sentiment. A sentiment, Stanley

thought, much at odds with the damning indictments she had – only moments before – cast over her fellow residents.

As she merrily took his drink order, the image of a chameleon came to mind, changing its appearance to hide within different environments.

Zara, he concluded, was a woman of many different faces.

(ii)

To: stanley_messina@PIservices.co.uk
From: TJ1989@datamail.com

RE: Investigation into death of George Thorpe

Dear Mr Messina. Or now that our paths have crossed, may I call you Stanley?

I have observed you spreading your net wide at Littleworth. Whilst your ability to make connections is commendable, I urge you not to be distracted by gossip or hearsay. The path to the truth, I believe, is littered with red herrings.

Sincerely,
Your Client

CHAPTER THIRTEEN

Stanley studied again the abstract painting that hung on the lounge wall of Riplingham Barn. He found that if he stood too close to it, the brushstrokes didn't make sense. Nothing more than a collection of lines and squiggles. But by taking a few steps back and looking at the artwork from a distance, the image of a male form burst into life with incredible vivacity. An artist capable of achieving such a feat must've possessed a natural talent. Not that such skill didn't demand self-discipline and practice, Stanley thought. Hours undoubtedly had been spent honing various techniques, experimenting with different genres and forms. The less-trodden path of the creative. Yet talent was undoubtedly required.

The painting, Stanley said to himself, had much in common with his investigation. It appeared to be made up of individual components, which presently criss-crossed one another in unexpected ways. A collection of dots that didn't connect to one another in any obvious pattern.

Perhaps, Stanley wondered, it was all a matter of perspective. Had he fallen into a trap of looking at the evidence too closely? Not taking the time to stand back to look at the bigger picture? He wasn't sure. He couldn't even be certain that he might be looking at everything from completely the wrong angle.

George Thorpe lay at the centre of this riddle. Wasn't that one certainty that Stanley could cling to? If his death hadn't been an accident, it was the culmination of prior events or deeds. Again, it returned to the notion of cause and effect.

In order to re-trace the sequence of events, Stanley re-told himself the story of George's history as simply as he could. From what he'd learnt, following the death of his partner Simeon Dean from a recreational drugs overdose, George had sold their warehouse apartment in London and relocated to Littleworth. His motive for moving out of the city appeared to be a conscious decision to remove himself from a lifestyle of excess and unhealthy behaviour. With a link to his sister already established in the location, Littleworth wasn't an entirely random choice. Quite the contrary. An obvious destination.

Once in residence at Riplingham Barn, George had explored an idea of creating a legacy for his deceased partner by planning to accept paying guests. However, from all suggestions, he'd approached his idea in a bullish manner, resulting in him being treated suspiciously as an outsider. Increasingly, he'd looked like a square peg in a round hole.

On the evening before his body was discovered, a gathering was held at The Plough to mark his niece's birthday. His behaviour by this stage had grown increasingly apparent. Stanley wasn't sure what word to describe it: distressed? provocative? angry? malicious? manic? The accounts he'd heard hadn't been conclusive. They might even be described as conflicting. Which only added a sense of murkiness to the whole business.

The next morning, George was discovered dead outside his home.

Stanley looked out again through the vast windows at the body of water, shimmering in the summer sunshine.

Something niggled him. It didn't feel quite right. What was it? Hadn't he laid out the sequence of events based on the facts?

He looked again at his notebook, where his jottings now filled many pages. He flicked through them as he paced back and forth across the flagstone floor. There, on an early page, was the list of names to which he'd added to since his time in Littleworth. Unless they could be entirely ruled out, they might all be considered suspects or potential witnesses. All persons of significant interest.

At the top of his initial list had been Bridget Heywood of whom Stanley had hoped to build a bridge into the community of Littleworth. He hadn't given up hope of still achieving this. For whilst progress had been slow, Stanley couldn't blame Bridget for being wary of him. He believed that her grief was genuine. Such emotions are difficult to fake, although not impossible. And yet, Bridget's refusal so far to openly share her spectacular fall from grace as a teacher because of a drugs conviction could demonstrate a propensity toward hiding other information. Information that might be crucial for solving this mystery. On the surface, of course, what troubled Stanley most was that Bridget appeared to have benefited from George's death. To inherit George's property looked to mark a shift in her, and her family's, fortune. Not too big a leap to wonder how they'd been impacted by her loss of career. Such an inheritance didn't automatically implicate her. Just something to consider.

Beneath Bridget's name was written Patrick's, who fair to say was still something of a stranger to Stanley bar the brief conversation they'd had at Downlands Farm. Apart from knowing that Patrick's family had moved to Littleworth following the death of his father in the pandemic, there was little else known about him thus far. On another page in his notebook, Stanley had written questions to himself regarding Patrick. What was Patrick's relationship with George like? Was his marriage to Bridget a happy one? What had he been doing for work before their move to Littleworth? What did he feel about Bridget's lost teaching career? There was one question he'd written that he now knew a little more about. What was his relationship like with his mother? In his own words, Patrick had described himself as the blue-eyed boy.

Stanley recalled the scene in the kitchen at Downlands Farm. He thought again of the blood. There'd definitely been tension between Joyce and her family. Stanley wagered that Joyce would hold opinions on what had happened to George. She hadn't struck him as the type of woman who held back on saying her piece.

That led to the next name on the list: Imogen Heywood. A young woman, of her own admission, who viewed Littleworth as a transitory place. Somewhere to be endured whilst waiting to move somewhere else. There had been a suggestion that she was at a crossroads in her life, still trying to work out which direction to take. She'd said herself that she'd been glad to have an opportunity to get to know George, the uncle who hadn't really been a big part of her life until then. His bohemian attitude had looked to sit well with her desire to be a writer. Perhaps he'd embodied a possibility that a creative life might be possible for her? But hadn't Zara Solomon at The Plough suggested that Imogen's parents might be protective of her? Hinting that perhaps George might've been a bad influence? Was there a limit to how far Imogen's family might be prepared to see her creative life stretch? Such are the things that cause family conflicts. Especially between different generations.

Next, of the residents who were present that evening in The Plough, were the occupants of Flint Cottage: Ursula Moor and her partner Quentin Ashcroft. Ursula, like Imogen, had apparently connected with George's personality, appreciating what he brought to the insular community. Stanley wondered whether this connection had manifested itself in any new-found creativity on Ursula's behalf? Was that how it worked for artists and writers? It was a mystery to Stanley where inspiration for such endeavours might spring from. It made him think again of Bridget laughing at his suggestion that George had been Simeon's muse. The idea had certainly tickled her. What he couldn't be sure of yet, was whether Ursula's friendship had caused any conflict with Quentin. And if so, why? He made a note to try and find out. In regards to Quentin, there was also the matter of his reluctance to see visitors on his doorstep. This had been alluded to on more than one occasion. A hint that he might be afraid of hippy-types rocking up next door. Again, it was another line of inquiry to pursue.

This left only Will and Zara Solomon, the owners of The Plough, of whom Stanley's speculations about them looked tenuous to say the least. They too had relocated to build a new life for themselves. An accident with a moped on a London street had curtailed a promising career in professional rugby. To think that George might be connected in some way to this incident required a stretch of the imagination. Stranger things have happened though, Stanley knew. Zara's own life story was all the evidence one needed to show how extraordinary things can occur. It made Stanley consider that perhaps George had realised the identities of The Plough's owners. But what benefit such knowledge might've been to him was unclear. Unless he sought to blackmail them, George didn't stand to profit from such knowledge. Besides, he didn't look to need the money, and from what Stanley had seen The Plough didn't appear an obvious cash

113

cow to exploit. Quite the opposite in fact. More apparently to be struggling financially since the pandemic.

Stanley looked again at the painting on the wall.

Was he missing something? All these fragments of information. Individual pieces of the investigation. Difficult to tell how, or if, the pieces might fit together. Were there still things out of sight that connected some of these elements in ways that he hadn't yet considered? Was he in danger of imagining potential links that might not exist?

For all his initial scouting for information, he felt deflated – downtrodden, even – that the investigation didn't look to have moved forward in any meaningful way. In some respects, his judgement felt more clouded now than it had at the beginning.

He continued to pace back and forth. He chastised himself for having been too soft in his approach. His concern for concealing his profession as a private investigator had prevented him from asking harder hitting questions. Too focused, perhaps, on merely blending into the environment. Trying not to raise suspicion in the minds of those around him.

Perhaps it was time to reconsider his approach? A shift from tentatively assessing how the land lay, to being more direct? It would be a risk. Doors may slam closed on him, or accusations thrown of raking things up again.

He thought of what Bridget had said. Her comment about a danger still being present.

Two questions loomed large in his mind.

Firstly, did he believe that George had been killed? And secondly, who was his client?

To the first question, Stanley had no idea. But to the second, he knew now that the client – unless they were deceiving him – lay in the circle of people he'd just examined. The odds on identifying this person had shifted in his favour. To get into the mind of this person could hold the key to it all. Their motivation might shed light on the more likely hidden connections between the names on his list. Until more details were known, he couldn't be sure that he wasn't being played with, like a cat does with a mouse. What harm might be done to his professional reputation if it turned out that the motives of his client weren't for the good?

Stanley made some further notes to himself in his notebook. He wrote down further lines of enquiry, and also some admonishments to himself. Stern reminders to keep his mind focused on the facts.

Having done so, he stopped and looked at the piece of paper lying on the worktop.

It was a handwritten note that he'd found on the doormat when he'd returned to Riplingham Barn from The Plough.

He wondered what had prompted it to be posted through the door.

He picked it up and re-read its brief contents. He would accept the invitation. But could it be, he wondered, that he was stepping further into the cat and mouse game?

CHAPTER FOURTEEN

Having been alone with his thoughts, Stanley was relieved to have a person to talk to.

'No need to apologise,' he said. 'I'll survive.'

'It's my fault. As I said, I should've arranged for it to be re-filled. What with everything going on, it slipped my mind.' Patrick frowned at the ugly green tank that housed the oil to service the barn. 'I've spoken to the delivery company on the phone, but they say their driver is fully booked for today.'

'It really isn't a problem.'

'Thanks for being so understanding. This is the type of thing that guests go and write reviews about online. Leaving a one-star rating. We have to be so careful. Bad reviews can sink a fledgling business.'

Stanley looked at the pond. There were other things that might deter potential visitors. Not just intermittent lack of hot water.

'What was your line of work before you came to Littleworth?' asked Stanley, thinking of the questions he'd written in his notebook.

Patrick folded his arms. 'It's a bit of a long story. A sorry saga.'

'Yes?'

Stanley sensed a reluctance on Patrick's behalf. The reason for the reticence wasn't apparent, but he was prepared to wait patiently for any potential disclosure.

'Looking back, it sounds flippant to say that I'd become tired of being a wage slave. I'd worked for many years as a chef in a hotel kitchen. The work in Eastbourne was steady and reliable, but I'd begun to feel unfulfilled by it.'

'So you decided to make a change?'

'That's it,' said Patrick. 'I decided to branch out on my own and run my own business – a restaurant. I thought my culinary experience would stand me in good stead. So I convinced Bridget that we should re-mortgage our home to finance it. She encouraged me and wanted to see me give it a go. We got swept up in the romance of it all.'

'I don't think you're the only ones to have pursued such a dream.'

'No, I suppose not. You see, I hadn't thought about how all the responsibility would fall on my shoulders. I knew I was an excellent chef, but all the other things that came with running a business were new to me. Finding reliable staff and juggling all the administrative side was a constant struggle. Do you know that twenty percent of new businesses fail within their first year? And that sixty percent fail within three years?'

Stanley hadn't known the exact figures but was aware of how difficult it was to start a new enterprise. The statistics, he guessed, were an explanation of where Patrick's description was heading.

'I was only just managing to keep my head above water. It was incredibly stressful. We'd invested so much money into it. I still wonder if it might've survived if it hadn't been for the pandemic. That was the straw that broke the camel's back. The custom dried up entirely. We weren't able to adapt quickly enough.'

'And it was at this time that your father died?'

Patrick nodded. 'It was a bad time. One misfortune after another.'

Stanley thought of Bridget's criminal conviction. The family had certainly endured their fair share of difficulties.

'We weren't sure whether moving to Littleworth was the right thing to do. But in the circumstances we found ourselves, there wasn't really another option. Of course, I was worried about how Bridget would find moving into my childhood home. I didn't think living with an in-law would be particularly helpful.'

'But Bridget came round to the idea?'

'I think it was George that swung it.'

'George?'

'Yes,' said Patrick. 'George said that he was enjoying life in Littleworth and that she might like it too. He hoped they'd get to reconnect with one another.'

Stanley wanted to be sure he'd heard correctly. 'You say George moved to Littleworth before you? I thought that he'd moved here to be closer to his sister?'

'Oh, you've got that round the wrong way. George was already living at Riplingham Barn when we moved to Downlands Farm.'

'I see,' said Stanley, already shifting in his mind the timeline he'd envisaged. It raised questions. Again, more *questions*. If Bridget hadn't been George's reason for moving to Littleworth, what had?

'It's funny how things work out, isn't it? Life never goes the way you think it might.' He was looking at the barn. Was there something unsaid in his expression? He looked like a man who'd been worn down by life. Someone, perhaps, whose dreams hadn't lived up to their expectations.

Having decided earlier to be more decisive in his questioning, Stanley seized the moment to clarify something that had been on his mind:

'You mentioned that you have an extra pair of hands at the farm? Somebody to help you with the manual labour?'

'Yes,' said Patrick. 'Jimbo.'

'He's the man with a beard? The man in the campervan on your land?'

'That's the one. Why do you ask?'

'I was just curious as to his story. You said that he won't stay forever? That he moves from place to place?'

'Jimbo's a bit of a mystery to us. He's a very private person. Keeps himself to himself.'

Stanley thought of the figure withdrawing into the van and closing the door behind him. Are those who are private, Stanley wondered, trying to hide something?

'I'd be interested to meet him,' said Stanley. Patrick

119

looked curiously at him. 'There's something about this place that makes me intrigued about other people. There's nothing like hearing a good story, is there?'

'No,' said Patrick. 'I don't suppose there is.'

Stanley knew that he was probably about to overstep the mark but decided to go for it anyway. 'What was *your* relationship like with George? Did you get on?'

'I wanted to get on with him. I really did. It's just that we were very different people. I wouldn't say that we *didn't* get on. Just that we both had completely different interests. There was no common ground between us. In fact, the only thing that linked us together was Bridget. And even then, their relationship was complicated.'

'Complicated?'

'Their upbringing wasn't easy.'

'Bridget told me that.'

'They relied on each other a lot. The bond between them was very strong, even when they were apart. They were siblings, but in some ways Bridget was maternal towards him. Trying to be the mother he'd never known.'

'Such strong relationships can leave others feeling left out or looking in from the outside.'

'Yes,' said Patrick. 'But that's not how I felt about it.'

Stanley wasn't sure. In the context of what he now knew about the Heywood's problems before moving to Littleworth, it was easy to see how the presence of Bridget's brother could've disturbed the balance. Had George upset the equilibrium of their marriage?

'You say Bridget was the only link between you and

George? What about Imogen? I believe she got on well with her uncle.'

'You've met my daughter. She's always been fiercely independent. I think in some ways she saw a lot of herself in George.'

'So you had no opinion on her relationship with him?'

'No,' said Patrick. 'Why should I? Imogen might've seen aspects of her creative nature in her uncle, but in other ways she wasn't like him at all. She's always had her head screwed on the right way. In that respect, she's more like her mother than her uncle. We've never had any concerns about her sense of judgement. I've never impressed my will upon her. It's important to let young people find their own way, don't you think?'

Stanley agreed. But he was curious as to the description of Bridget's judgement. It brought to mind the incident that had destroyed her teaching career. The two didn't sit comfortably together.

'George's death was a sorry accident,' said Patrick. 'I think we've all wondered whether, with hindsight, we should've done anything different. As if changing something might've altered the ultimate conclusion. It's probably only natural to think about such things, eh? But what's done is done now.'

Not for the first time, Stanley sensed that George's death had scarred the small community. It was a wound that might take a long time to heal. It's impact sending out waves, like ripples on the surface of that pond.

Patrick reassured Stanley again that the delivery of

oil would be made as soon as possible. It was an oversight, he repeated. His mind had been full of other things.

As Stanley walked up the garden path towards the door surrounded by a pretty climbing rose, another theory began to formulate in his mind. He looked at the neat borders enclosed by the picket fence. If only his thoughts could be as ordered. Perhaps then some clarity might emerge from the muddle. It was Patrick that had got him thinking again that perhaps he'd been looking at everything from completely the wrong direction. What Patrick said had made him re-evaluate the whole sequence of events.

By coincidence, as he reached the door and lifted his hand to knock, it opened at exactly that moment.

Quentin couldn't hide his surprise at finding the visitor on his doorstep. 'I was just going out for a walk,' he said. 'I always go for a walk at this time of the afternoon.'

A man of routine, Stanley thought. *Always*, is a strong word.

'Oh, don't let me stop you,' said Stanley as he pulled the note from his pocket. He didn't unfold it. 'Ursula invited me round for afternoon tea.'

There was an undisguised flash of incomprehension on the man's face before it returned to an implacable mask of civility. For a second, Quentin looked unsure as to whether to continue out on his afternoon constitution or abandon the walk to step back into Flint Cottage.

'That's the type of thing Ursula does,' he said. 'Making visitors feel welcome. Always thinking of other people.'

Clearly, she hadn't told Quentin about the invitation.

'You better come in,' said Quentin, stepping aside to let him into the hallway. 'Ursula!' he called. 'Ursula, are you there? We have a visitor…'

He heard her before he could see her. Her shoes appeared at the top of the staircase. As she descended, he thought again of a little bird.

'Oh, Stanley. It's you. How nice to see you.'

'Afternoon tea?' said Quentin.

'Why, of course,' she replied, in such a way that sounded as if she'd forgotten entirely.

Did Stanley detect a flutter of frustration in Quentin's manner? A suggestion that perhaps Ursula was inclined to be forgetful. Hadn't she herself said that she was often away with the fairies? Daydreaming about fantasy characters, settings, and plots for her novels.

'I'll leave you to it,' said Quentin, opting to stick with his afternoon routine rather than join them for tea.

The choice, Stanley noted, hadn't been an easy one.

Stanley watched the front door close.

'Let's not stand on ceremony,' said Ursula brightly. 'Come in. Come in…'

CHAPTER FIFTEEN

Stanley had placed Ursula high on his list of people who might be his mystery client. Ever since he'd met her in the walled kitchen garden, he'd wondered whether she'd been lingering that day in the hope of bumping into him. Harvesting may have been a convincing ruse.

Her handwritten note inviting him to afternoon tea also suggested that she was keen to speak with him further. Although Quentin saying that such an invite was simply typical of her character reminded him not to jump to any conclusions. Apart from reports of Ursula striking up a friendship with George, there were no other indications of why she might suspect somebody had killed him.

'I hope it hasn't impacted upon your stay at Riplingham Barn? You know, what happened to George and everything.'

She flittered around the tiny kitchen.

Her opening gambit did little to shake his feelings about the potential of her being his employer.

She continued: 'Unfortunate that you should stay just after the outcome of the inquest was announced.

Having it reported in the news sort of stirred everything up again. Just when we thought it might be going away, people started talking about it all over again.'

'It's a significant thing to have happened in a small place.'

'Exactly.'

'I suppose it's inevitable that the actual location of George's death was bound to come under scrutiny. Maybe it's become almost a shrine to him.'

'I hadn't thought of it like that,' she said as she placed cups and saucers on a tray. 'It would be a shame for him to be remembered mainly by the place that he died. Especially in light of it being such a nasty accident.'

'It's funny you should say that. Bridget said something similar about George's partner.'

Ursula poured boiling water into an elaborate teapot. Steam billowed into the air.

'His partner was an artist,' she said. 'From what I understand he struggled with his creativity. George didn't like to talk about it much. I think it was too raw for him. But I suspected from his curiosity into my own creative processes that he was interested in artistic minds.'

'I suppose it can't be easy. Maybe lonely at times?' He thought of his own profession. It too brought with it a sense of isolation at times. He wondered whether there were any other parallels to be drawn.

'They had each other, George and Simeon. Just as I have Quentin. I think it helps. To have someone there to encourage. To support you unconditionally.'

'Yes, that makes a lot of sense.'

Ursula reached up to a cupboard and lifted down an ancient looking biscuit tin. She opened it and laid pink wafers out on a plate. The whole afternoon tea was contained upon a rickety looking tray.

'What was it that Bridget said about it?'

'She said that George wanted to create a legacy for Simeon and his work. For him to be remembered by something other than the circumstances in which he'd died. She told me of his plan to welcome visitors to stay at Littleworth.'

'That's right,' said Ursula.

'Can you tell me any more about his idea?'

'There's not much more to it than you've outlined. From what he told me, he had a concept of bringing groups of creative folk together so that they could share their experiences. Being creative can be lonely at times, so he thought people would find it beneficial. I think he saw it as a way of doing something positive with the proceeds of Simeon's artwork.'

Stanley again thought that the idea had merit.

'Bridget said that George saw the idea as a form of storytelling? Was that something he discussed with you?'

'We talked about a lot of things. He was very easy to talk to. I've come to see through my writing the power that storytelling holds. It has the potential to heal. I thought that his idea was a good one. But I don't think that was his primary objective in discussing his plans with me.'

'No?'

Ursula lifted the tray from the worktop. 'Let's go through to the sitting room.'

They moved through the cramped hallway into the room at the front of the cottage. The afternoon sunshine shone through the old windows. It illuminated the room in sepia tones. Everything in the space, from the armchairs to the pictures on the wall, looked faded. It was shabby and tatty in a comfortable lived-in way.

Ursula put the tray down on a coffee table and they both sat down.

'Did Bridget mention to you about the shepherd huts?'

'Yes,' said Stanley. 'They were where George intended to house his guests.'

'That's right. He described them as storytelling huts. From what I could gather, they weren't going to be like traditional camping. He was going to fit them out to be cosy and modern. A little optimistic to say they'd be luxurious, but you get my drift.'

Stanley thought of the barn and the narrow lane that led up to it. He pictured the pond and the walled garden. The question he then asked was an obvious one: 'But where did George envisage these storytelling huts being located? I can't think of an obvious place.'

'There's a strip of land that runs out behind us at Flint Cottage. It belongs to Downlands Farm and butts up against the boundary of Riplingham Barn. It sits just behind the walled garden.'

Stanley hadn't ventured beyond the walled garden,

but from what he recalled it didn't look to be immediately appropriate. 'Isn't it very overgrown there?'

'It's become that way, yes. Although it wasn't always the case. It used to be one of the less-trodden paths out of the village. That was until things started to get on top of Doug and Joyce. Latterly, they had to restrict the amount of clearing they did each year, to concentrate on the jobs that mattered most.'

'So technically the land belonged to Downlands Farm?'

'It still does. The plan was for George to buy the section of land from them and clear the space to locate the storytelling huts. From what he said, not only would this achieve his plan, it would also help the farm with their finances. But when George died there was no longer a desire to follow through with his plans. And the money Bridget inherited took away I suppose the incentive to sell. The barn was an incredible asset, let alone its revenue potential.'

'That still doesn't explain why George was keen to discuss the idea of the huts with you?'

'I was just getting to that. You see, George realised that even if he could purchase the land from Downlands Farm, he would still require planning permission to site the huts there. Some people thought that George went at things like a bull at a gate, but he was more canny than that. He saw that the only people likely to object to the planning application would be us, Quentin and me.'

'So he thought if he could get you on side he'd more

likely have success with a planning application?'

'Butter us up, you mean. I'm not sure it was quite as black and white as that. I just think he saw the potential difficulty of the situation.' She looked to be choosing her words carefully. 'I think he guessed that any objection wouldn't come from me.'

'Meaning it was more likely to be Quentin?'

Ursula sipped her tea. It seemed that she might be tight-lipped on this topic, but as the cup returned to her saucer she proceeded to elaborate: 'Quentin isn't always the easiest of people to get on with. Often, people don't understand him. I don't mean in what he says. Just in terms of his manner and outlook on life.'

Stanley thought of the initial conversation he'd had with Quentin over the picket fence. He recalled how he'd concluded that this was a man who found difficult to embrace change.

'When you've lived with someone for so long,' said Ursula, 'you become blind to how they might come across to others. I suppose you might say that the pair of us have become co-dependent. And I don't say that as if it's a bad thing. We sort of level one another out. I'm a daydreamer. I love to fantasise about the bigger picture. Sometimes I get lost in my imagination entirely. Whereas Quentin is practical and steadfast. He enjoys routine and keeping things in order.'

Stanley recalled the pride in which Quentin had spoken of looking after Ursula's business and administrative affairs. The success of her books looked to have been the result of a constructive partnership.

'You sound like very different people. Isn't it said

129

that opposites attract?'

Ursula smiled. 'That's true. Although I must confess that it was his dashing good looks that first caught my eye. He was very handsome.'

'How did you meet?'

She looked wistfully towards the window as she recalled their coming together. A glimmer of something slightly sad looking appeared in her eyes as she spoke. A sense of it all being a little bittersweet. 'Quentin was married at the time. His wife's name was Nancy. They too worked together. Nancy was a little older than Quentin. They met just as Nancy was completing her degree in literature, and Quentin was about to pursue his own higher education studies in medicine. It was a party of a mutual friend. One of those parties that you don't really think about much, but then bump into someone who changes the course of your life.

'Nancy was extraordinarily ambitious and driven. I suppose they were both young and had the energy for it all then. It was her idea to set up a publishing house and she convinced Quentin to abandon his ambitions of medicine to help build the business. They began in a small office in south London. They got married and soon had a baby; a daughter named Skye.'

'Was the business a success?'

'I think that depends on how you look at it. Financially, it was making a small return and it had a growing reputation with readers and authors. But on a personal level, it took a toll on them both. The lines between work and family life got blurred. Nancy wanted to see the business get to the next level which required further commitment on their behalf. Quentin sort of found himself a little side-lined. Being left in Nancy's shadow. Which, I think, made him rather regret his decision to abandon the career in medicine he'd once imagined.'

Ursula blinked. Did her eyes look ever so watery?

'It was because Quentin was trying to find a niche for himself that he focused his attention on scouring the unsolicited manuscripts that got sent to them. He thought that discovering a successful author would prove he had an eye for spotting talent. I'm sorry. I'm rather rambling. You've probably guessed where this story goes?'

'One of your manuscripts was in his pile?'

'Got it in one. I'd sent it out countless times to larger more established publishers. To be honest, I was on the verge of abandoning the whole idea. I'd almost given up hope.'

'But Quentin saw something in it.'

'Yes,' she said. 'He asked to meet me. I thought he was sensitive and kind towards my writing. The amendments he suggested were helpful. And when we reached a stage of agreeing upon a contract I felt that he had my best interests at heart. I felt I could trust him. An important thing for a writer.'

'It became more than a professional working relationship though?' It wasn't easy to envisage Ursula in the role of *other woman*.

'I was hardly a scarlet woman, if that's what you're thinking. It wasn't as if I was his mistress or anything.

131

His marriage had hit the rocks long before I came along. We just sort of clicked. We tried to make things as amicable as we could, for Skye's sake as much as anything. I didn't want to be the evil stepmother.'

The potted history of Ursula and Quentin's relationship had been interesting, but Stanley wanted to be sure of its implications in relation to his own investigation. 'So, you said that people don't always understand Quentin?'

'Quentin's very protective of those closest to him. I think that often gets mistaken for being a stick in the mud.'

'And you say *you* had no objection to the idea of the storytelling huts?'

Ursula shook her head. 'Not at all. George was very up with new ideas. We discussed how the guests might be interested in where I write and my writing process. He thought it would provide an opportunity to sell more books, which sounded logical to me. People are often curious about *how* writers work, don't you think?'

She appeared to be seeking affirmation. To have it confirmed that the idea she'd discussed with George had been realistic.

Stanley grasped the moment. 'Would you show me where you write? Or is that overstepping the mark?'

Ursula's face lit up. 'Not at all,' she said, putting down her teacup and getting eagerly to her feet. 'Let me show you.'

She was quick to lead the way. Through the hallway and up the creaking narrow staircase. At the top, they paused on the landing where they looked at the doors to the four rooms. One stood slightly ajar to reveal an antiquated bathroom. Another, in which there was a double bed covered with a quilt, was hers and Quentin's bedroom.

'We have a room each to work in,' Ursula explained. She looked to her left. 'This room here is my writing room. Come and have a look. You'll see there's nothing magical about it.'

She was correct. Stanley was struck by how sparse the little room was. It contained a small armchair, a desk with a chair, and a wooden bookcase with some reference books and all her published titles. Her name was clear on all the spines.

'I sit at the desk and write everything by hand. Then Quentin types up the words on to a computer before handing a draft back for me to edit. We've always worked that way. It made George laugh. He said that I could've worked quicker if I'd typed the words myself. But I explained to him, there's something about holding a pen in my hand. The words come easier that way. And besides, I'm a little superstitious about it all. If it isn't broken, don't fix it.'

George had clearly shown an interest in Ursula and her writing. Stanley supposed it had echoes of George's relationship with Simeon Dean.

A small cork pinboard hung above her meagre desk. On it was a calendar on which days had been ticked off, presumably as part of her writing regime. There were also an array of greetings card attached to the boards with pins, some of which now curled at the edges and had faded so badly the pictures on them could barely be seen.

'Ah, those are birthday cards sent to me from Skye – Quentin's daughter. She has always been a thoughtful girl. A woman now, of course.'

'You are close?'

Ursula ran her hand across the back of her desk chair thoughtfully. 'She always sends me a card on my birthday. She never forgets.'

It was hardly a conclusive answer, but Stanley sensed that the topic might be off limits.

Stanley glanced again at the greeting cards. He did a quick count of the number. They must've been important to Ursula for her to have kept them so long. And yet, she didn't strike him as a particularly sentimental person.

'Quentin works in his office over there,' said Ursula.

'May I look?'

She looked uncertain, anxious even. 'He's very private about his workspace, but as he's not here we could just pop our heads in.'

She led him the small distance almost on tiptoes.

Quentin's room was a stark contrast to Ursula's. The curtains half-drawn. Stacks of paper and magazines and newspapers looked to be that of a hoarder. Amongst the mountains of clutter, there was a dated computer. It looked chunky and yellow. Beside the dusty keyboard lay a well-thumbed edition of *The Writers' and Artists' Yearbook*.

'It's organised chaos,' said Ursula. 'He knows where everything is. There isn't a review, interview or write-up of my books that isn't in here somewhere. I'm grateful for it all. I don't think I could concentrate on my writing if I had to look after all the business-side myself.' She scanned the cluttered room. 'I think it might've startled Imogen somewhat.'

'Imogen?'

'Yes,' said Ursula. 'You know that she wants to be a writer too? She has a lot of talent. She asked whether she could spend a week doing work experience with us. It's her gap year. She thought it might look good on her CV.'

'She spent a week with you? When was this?'

'Oh, some time before Christmas. The poor girl got a nasty germ half-way through the week so was only with us a couple of days in the end. I'm not sure how useful she found it.'

'May I ask you a question?'

'Of course,' said Ursula. 'Ask me anything.'

Stanley pulled the handwritten note from his pocket and unfolded it. 'Was there a reason for asking me here today?'

Her face was blank. She looked uncomprehendingly at the scrap of paper in his hand. 'What do you mean?' She reached out and took the note. She saw the invitation and her own name. 'I'm sorry, Stanley. There must be some kind of misunderstanding. I didn't write this. It's not from me.'

Her words halted at the sound of a key being put in the front door.

Stanley's heart sank. He suspected that Quentin's return would curtail Ursula's openness. Was that a flash of terror in her eyes? 'Let's not mention this to him,' she whispered. 'Okay?'

CHAPTER SIXTEEN

There was something in the way Quentin said, 'Anyone at home?' that sounded artificial. He knew all too well that Ursula would be there. It made Stanley wonder how often Ursula ventured out of the house. Was the walled garden next door a potential escape for her? Somewhere to seek sanctuary?

'We're upstairs,' said Ursula, tugging at Stanley's sleeve so that they would be visible at the top of the staircase. 'I was showing Stanley where I write.'

Quentin didn't reply.

What did the silence mean?

The walls of the cottage suddenly seemed to encroach. Stanley followed Ursula as she blustered her way downstairs. He thought again of a little bird, but this time with its wings flapping. Was Flint Cottage, he wondered, a cage in which she lived?

He surreptitiously slipped the note he'd shown her back into his pocket. Her denial at having written it had appeared genuine. Which raised the possibilities that either she was extremely forgetful, or more likely that it had been written by someone else. But by whom? Stanley wondered. And why?

'You didn't walk for very long today,' said Ursula to Quentin as she and Stanley reached the bottom of the stairs. The space felt very cramped for the three of them.

'The sun is fierce out there. It's very hot, and I didn't want to get burnt.'

It was a reasonable explanation. More likely though, thought Stanley, that he'd been eager to get home to check on Ursula and her guest.

'Let me get another cup from the kitchen,' said Ursula. 'The tea will still be warm and I'm sure there's another cup to be squeezed from the pot.' As she went to the kitchen, Quentin and Stanley took a seat wordlessly in the sitting room. Quentin looked pensively at his hands. He seemed preoccupied. He sat rigidly upright. 'Here we are,' said Ursula returning with a cup and saucer.' The formality of it all suggested a couple unfamiliar with having visitors. She lifted the teapot and poured. 'Let me be mother.'

Had Stanley caught a flinch on Quentin's behalf?

'Ursula was telling me about her writing process,' said Stanley. 'And the part you play in it.'

'Was she.'

'Yes,' said Ursula. 'You know, how we divide the creative and the administrative aspects between us. He is interested in it. Won't you tell him about what you do?'

Quentin gave a little sniff. He raised his nose as if to accentuate the importance of his part in the process. 'I'm the bridge between Ursula and the publishers, you might say. It's not easy for any writer to get a contract, so with each book it's almost back to square one again.'

'What does that actually involve?'

'It's an ongoing process of *querying*. I send out the first two chapters of the manuscript with a synopsis of the whole novel. It can take months for anything to be read, so not only do I send a stamped addressed envelope for return of submission if not suitable for their list, I also enclose another one for them to acknowledge immediate receipt.'

'Imagine waiting for months for a response,' said Ursula, 'only to discover that the manuscript had never reached them in the first place.'

'It sounds like a slow process.'

'It requires patience and persistence,' said Quentin sagely.

Ursula gave a wan smile. 'Us talking of George,' she said to Stanley, 'reminds me that he thought it was funny how Quentin and I worked. He used to laugh at us, didn't he?'

Quentin didn't answer.

'He said that it was like we were stuck in a time warp,' she continued. 'Like we were insects encased in amber. He said that *nobody* sent hard copies of manuscripts to publishers in this day and age. That everything should be sent electronically through the computer.'

'What would he have known? Had George ever published a book?'

'He just said…'

'George said… George said… That's all I ever heard. George Thorpe was a self-appointed expert on *everything*. There wasn't a topic that he wasn't prepared to give his opinion on.'

Ursula looked embarrassed. 'Oh, I don't think that's very fair. His intentions were good.'

'He was an agitator. He enjoyed stirring the pot.'

Ursula straightened her skirt. Her manner suggested that she held some qualms at talking ill of the dead. 'Maybe so, but underneath it all he cared for those close to him. It was he who suggested Imogen come and do work experience with us. Because he wanted the best for her.'

Quentin huffed.

'Even the birthday party for Imogen was George's idea.'

'And look how that turned out.'

'We couldn't have foreseen George's accident,' she said.

'We should never have gone to the pub that night. It was a silly idea.'

An invisible strain seemed to pull between them, something deep and unresolved. It was as if they'd forgotten Stanley was present at all.

'What made you go to Imogen's party?' asked Stanley, bringing himself back into the conversation.

'Yes,' said Quentin. 'What made us?'

Ursula frowned. 'I like Imogen. I see a lot of myself in her. That's why I agreed for her to come and do work experience with us. I'd felt disappointed that her illness had cut short her time with us. It was so long since anyone had invited us to a party, the idea appealed to me. Selfish reasons, I suppose.'

'Selfish?' said Stanley.

'Well, it was my birthday the following day too. Quentin doesn't believe in astrology, but I've always been a little bit of a believer. Might there be something in Imogen and I having similar interests? I wasn't going to tell anyone, as it was Imogen's celebration, but I couldn't help liking the idea of vicariously marking my own birthday too with a village gathering.'

There was something sad about her story. It suggested things that had been denied. A regret at missing out.

'I really just wanted to see a cake and hear Happy Birthday being sung,' said Ursula. 'Does that sound silly?'

'No,' said Stanley. He tried to picture the residents all together at The Plough. 'Was there a cake? Was there singing?'

'Oh yes,' she replied. 'Zara made a beautiful cake. She brought it out from the kitchen covered with candles, and we all sang Happy Birthday. Do you remember, Quentin?'

Quentin nodded. His eyes looked like glass.

'Zara insisted that Imogen make a wish as she blew out the candles,' said Ursula.

Quentin gave a quick gasp. Stanley saw him bite his bottom lip.

'Quentin?' said Ursula. 'Are you okay? What is it?'

'Just what you said. Just then. It brought something back to me. Something I'd forgotten about entirely.'

'About that evening?'

'Yes,' he said. 'That moment you described when

141

Imogen blew out the candles. It was thinking of the flames and the smoke. And the look on Imogen's face as she made a wish. She'd looked around when she'd done it, as if trying to spot someone. Don't you remember?'

'No,' said Ursula.

'I remember thinking at the time that she was looking for someone. And when I scanned the room, there was somebody missing.'

'There was someone missing?' she said. 'But who? Who wasn't there?'

CHAPTER SEVENTEEN

Alone, in the silence of the barn, surrounded by the lingering spirit of George Thorpe, Stanley's head was full the voices of Littleworth's residents, each giving an opinion on their version of events.

Stanley thought of the night George had died. He pictured the snowstorm, so vividly described by those who had gathered in The Plough that evening. It felt, thought Stanley, that the blizzard had never really ended. The snow may have melted long ago, but the distortion brought by those falling flakes still remained.

Not for the first time, Stanley worried that he was in danger of looking in the wrong direction. To pursue an avenue that might ultimately lead to a dead end.

His time at Flint Cottage the previous afternoon had raised more questions than answers. Such seemed to be the way in this investigation. It was like pulling at a tiny loose thread only to discover that in doing so a series of other threads became apparent, unravelling in unexpected ways. Ursula's insistence that she'd not written the note inviting him to afternoon tea played heavily on his mind. As he'd thought at the time, either she had a terrible memory – which seemed highly implausible based on his initial impressions of her – or, which troubled him more, somebody else had written it. Somebody willing to manipulate him. Move him around like a toy.

He didn't like it.

Neither was he content with Quentin's account of the evening at The Plough. What he'd said about the moment Imogen had blown out her candles once again raised doubts. Had those he'd spoken to about that night been entirely honest? Or were their memories unreliable?

He was going round in circles.

The little pages of his notebook were no longer sufficient to contain his theories on the case. Thinking again of the blizzard, he spent lost hours ripping out pages and laying them out across the floor with more detailed notes scribbled on them. His aim, in doing so, was to identify all the disparate elements and hope to establish any potential links between them. To be led by the evidence.

It wasn't a game, but in some ways it felt like one. Battling against an invisible foe. A twisted game of hide and seek. With the possible perpetrator hidden in clear sight.

It would do no good to pursue things in an unconsidered way. No, he decided, he would spend the day thinking about his next move, like pondering pieces on his chess board. Where should he go next? And what would the implications of such a move be?

The next morning, after breakfast, Stanley locked the door of Riplingham Barn and set off purposefully down the lane. His deliberations of the previous day had settled into a considered next move. What the outcome of this decision might be, of course, he wasn't sure. To feel that he was calling the shots, however, rather than being manipulated by any third party, buoyed him with a sense of optimism.

There was always a chance that the conclusions he'd drawn might be wrong. He might still be looking in the wrong direction. However, as he strode between the hedgerows, the cogs continued to turn confidently in his brain. From all those conflicting stories, some likely ideas were beginning to emerge.

As he emerged from the lane, Stanley noticed a taxi at the gate of Flint Cottage. Its engine was idling. Its presence stood out in the sleepiness of that Littleworth morning. Too early even for the first ramblers heading to the downs. Even the parasols on the tables outside The Plough hadn't yet been raised.

He passed the taxi with a small greeting to the driver who replied with a genial nod.

Walking on towards his destination, the cogs continued to turn.

At the rusty entrance gates to Downlands Farm, he glanced surreptitiously back at the vehicle to see one of the rear passenger doors closing. He hadn't seen who had got in, but he had a good idea who it had been.

He continued his gradual ascent towards the farmhouse. The land upon which it surveyed stretched out towards the rolling hills, verdant and green in the summer morning. He noticed that the air was abuzz with bumblebees and other insects. Butterflies fluttered here and there.

The campervan he'd seen before hadn't moved from its spot. Its door was closed, and curtains drawn. Impossible to tell whether its occupant was within or not. But this wasn't where he was going.

Instead, he approached the front door of the farmhouse and lifted the heavy knocker on it. He gave a decisive knock. As he waited for an answer, a quick look back over his shoulder revealed that the taxi had gone. It must've turned and headed back up the road that Stanley had driven into Littleworth.

The door opened warily. He saw her face peer out of the crack from the shadows.

'Oh,' she said, 'it's you.'

She pulled the door wider with a creak.

'Patrick's out with the animals,' she said. 'And Bridget's working up at the summer house.'

Stanley noticed the bandage on Joyce's arm. The wound was taking time to heal.

'It was actually you I was hoping to speak with,' he said.

'Me? What would you want to speak to me about?'

'May I come in? I would like to speak to you in private.'

She looked reluctant, but with an almost imperceivable shrug of her tiny shoulders, she opened the door to him.

They moved to the kitchen, where Joyce closed the

door behind them. Her ragged face scrutinised him as she eased herself upon her chair. She pointed to where Stanley should sit at the kitchen table. 'Well?' she grunted. 'What is it? What do you have to say?'

He preluded his point with a brief explanation. 'I work as a private investigator. I'm currently employed by a client who has reason to believe that George Thorpe's death may not have been an accident.'

Stanley looked at her closely for any reaction to his words, but she barely moved. 'Not an accident?' she said eventually, her hand moving slowly up to cradle the arm which had the bandage on it. 'Do you mean that it might've been deliberate?'

'Yes,' said Stanley. 'That's exactly what I mean.'

She suddenly appeared very forthright in her posture. Whilst being old, she clearly still had strength, both mental and physical.

'When will it ever end?' she said. 'That man brought nothing but ill fortune to Littleworth. He's like a shadow hanging over us. Even now. He was a bad omen. Isn't it time for us to be able to move on?'

It wasn't the first time such a sentiment had been expressed. A keenness to bury the past and move on.

'If George was killed, don't you think he deserves justice?'

'If…' she said. '*If*…'

'You don't believe it?'

'When you're as old as me, you come to realise that life doesn't always dovetail neatly together. Sometimes bad things happen for no particular reason. They just do. Looking for explanations when they might not exist only ever results in getting tied up in knots. Life should be lived moving forward, not stuck in a loop.'

Stanley wasn't sure that she'd answered his question. She'd swerved it.

'If I can ascertain the facts,' he said, 'then perhaps I can help everyone involved achieve a sense of closure.'

She didn't answer. Nor did she look convinced.

'On the evening before George's body was discovered, there was a gathering held at The Plough for Imogen's birthday.' As Stanley spoke, he noticed her push her knees together fiercely. Her whole body appeared to tense. 'Everybody from Littleworth, I understand, was there. Except you?'

'Imogen asked me to go. I said that she wouldn't want an old fuddy duddy like me there. But it was the weather that made my mind up. The snow was coming down heavy. I didn't want to be out in the cold or risk slipping over. Accidents at my age can be fatal,' she said, clutching her bandage for effect.

Stanley listened but wasn't sure how true her words sounded. Joyce Heywood, he thought, was not the type of woman to be put off by a bit of snow.

'You stayed here at the farmhouse?'

She looked at him through white lashes. 'Yes,' she said.

'But you weren't alone all evening, were you?'

He saw from her instant reaction that his calculated gamble had paid off.

'He was drunk,' said Joyce. 'Or high on some kind of drugs.'

'George?'

'Yes,' she said. 'He banged on the front door, yelling and shouting.'

Stanley recalled Quentin's description of Imogen blowing out the candles on her cake. She'd looked around after making a wish for her uncle. But he hadn't been there.

'He'd slipped away from the party?' asked Stanley.

'Must've done. He'd stormed up here, reeking of booze.'

'What was he shouting about?'

Joyce lowered her head a little. 'It hadn't been easy for me, either. I'd not long lost my husband. I don't think people were seeing it from that perspective. They weren't seeing that it was difficult for me too.'

Stanley didn't push her. He waited quietly for her to explain further.

'With hindsight, I should've done things differently,' she continued. 'I should've thought about how it was for her as well as me.'

'Do you mean Bridget?' Stanley asked, taking a punt.

'Yes,' she said. 'George was angry that I hadn't been more accommodating when Bridget had moved to Downlands Farm. He accused me of making her life a misery. He said that I played favourites with Patrick. He told me that I should've been grateful for all Bridget had given up for me. He called me a selfish old bitch. Said that I was bitter and twisted. Said that Doug would've been ashamed of me. Which really stung. How would he know? I said that he'd never even met Doug...'

Her mini tirade had left her slightly breathless.

'From what I've learnt,' said Stanley, 'George was protective of his sister, and vice versa.'

'That's the way of families, isn't it?'

'I suppose so. Did you think George was being fair to you?'

'It's not always easy to admit that you're in the wrong. I reflected on what George said. Perhaps I *had* been caught up in my own viewpoint. I tried to change my ways after that. Tried to be more accommodating.'

'Was that all he said?' asked Stanley.

'He wasn't here very long. I don't think he wanted to be missed at the party. Didn't want Bridget to know that he'd come and said his piece.'

'And there was nothing else he mentioned that might suggest potential conflict with anyone else that evening?'

'No,' said Joyce. 'He was stumbling over his words. Kept rambling to me about being betrayed by supposed loved ones, as if he was determined to ram home the point about how he'd thought I treated Bridget.'

Betrayed by supposed loved ones?

Stanley could see how Joyce might've taken those words to heart, but wondered whether they could've been spoken in a wider context?

He didn't think that Joyce was lying to him, but he wasn't sure that she'd told him the whole story.

He might've been inclined to pursue his questioning with more fervour if it hadn't been for his attention being drawn to the crack between the kitchen door and the floor. A movement had caught his eye. Somebody had been outside, listening no doubt to their conversation. Only the drifting away of a lingering shadow remained of the unknown person's presence…

CHAPTER EIGHTEEN

Stanley stepped back out into the sunshine, relieved to escape the confines of the farmhouse. He breathed the fresh air into his lungs. It couldn't have been easy for them all to have moved under the same roof. He tried to see it from all their perspectives, to be sympathetic to each of them.

He pulled the door closed behind him, thoughtfully.

No, it must have been a challenge. For each of them to be processing their own loss and grief in such close quarters. Being under such pressure must've magnified their emotions and feelings, with some being repressed and avoided whilst others boiled over in the type of situation Joyce had outlined. It was, perhaps, the type of environment in which regrettable things could be spoken in the heat of the moment. Simmering tensions cranked up to a level that they might explode into impulsive reactions.

Hyperbole, Stanley chastised himself. These ideas were merely speculation.

Having now consciously revealed his profession to another Littleworth resident, he began to feel a weight of time passing upon him. The clock was ticking. Soon his identity would be known by all those around him, with no more opportunities to fly undetected under the radar.

He was keen to move his thought processes on to reflecting and analysing Joyce's account of that evening and her exchange with George. There were some elements that required further examination. But his ponderings were interrupted by an approaching presence at his heels. He sensed her before he saw her.

'I saw you leave,' she said. Her dark locks made her look paler than the last time he'd seen her. 'I've got some books to put in the book exchange. I'll walk with you.'

'Of course,' he replied.

'You're a private investigator then?'

Stanley wasn't surprised. He'd suspected that Imogen had been the person beyond the closed door. Something about the spritely manner in which the shadow had moved.

'You listened to our conversation?' he asked.

'Oh, there's not much point in trying to keep secrets in Littleworth. The walls have ears here. Everyone knows everyone's business.'

'So it seems,' said Stanley.

'Bit of a dark horse, though. Gran, I mean. Her having George come and shout at her that evening, but not tell a soul about it.'

They ambled along.

'Did you notice that George wasn't in The Plough?' he asked, choosing not to reveal that Quentin had given his own version of events.

'Yes,' she said. 'I probably wouldn't have noticed, or remembered, but it was because I blew out the candles. They'd made me a cake for my birthday, you see. Somebody said that I should make a wish.'

'And you did?'

'It'll sound sentimental, but I wished that George would be happy. He said that he wasn't sure he'd ever find love again, which sounded very sad. I didn't want him to be lonely. I wanted him to be happy. So you can understand why I looked around for him after making such a wish. But he wasn't there.'

'You didn't know he'd come to the farm?'

'No,' she said. 'I don't suppose anyone did. I remember seeing George again later that evening. I can't remember exactly when. I think I'd assumed that perhaps he'd gone outside for a cigarette. It didn't really seem very important.'

Stanley wasn't sure. Sometimes the way through the woods lay in the smallest of details. In the things that might be overlooked. Things that could be mistaken as trivial details that didn't matter.

Imogen asked him the question that Joyce hadn't: 'Who's asked you to investigate George's death? Who thinks it wasn't an accident?'

Stanley saw no point in lying to her. 'I don't know. They haven't told me who they are.'

He thought he saw her sweep a quick gaze across vista. 'Somebody here?'

'Yes,' he said.

The conversation faltered. He noticed that she clutched the books she carried tightly to her chest. He sensed that she was thinking, but what about he couldn't decipher. It was as if she was contemplating whether to tell him something. On the verge of opening up to him, to make some possible revelation.

'Stanley!' a voice called. They both looked in its direction to where Patrick was bounding across to them, waving his mobile phone in the air. 'I've just had a call from the oil company. The delivery driver will be with you this afternoon. You'll have hot water again!'

'Thank you,' said Stanley, simultaneously grateful for the prospect of warm water, but cursing at having been interrupted. From the way Imogen peeled away from them as Patrick approached, Stanley realised that the moment had passed. She was walking away with her books, and anything that she might have been about to say.

Stanley returned to the notes he'd laid out on the lounge floor of Riplingham Barn. He felt pleased that his calculated guess as to where George had gone to had proved to be correct, but curious that he wasn't confident that Joyce had shared with him the whole picture.

Once more, through questioning and listening, Stanley moved a little nearer to understanding George Thorpe. The investigation continued to reveal aspects of his personality and character, with this latest tale exposing the fierce loyalty he had to Bridget. Just as he'd seemed determined to protect Simeon Dean's legacy, so too did he appear to want to shelter his sister. Again, Stanley reflected that crimes are often the consequence of love rather than hate.

The cogs in his brain turned again.

On rare occasions, Stanley stopped to think about what had led him to his profession. He didn't like to dwell on it too much, as the memories were complex and painful. It followed him around nonetheless, like a speck in the corner of his eye. He feared that in unpacking his own past, the confronting aspects of who he'd been and what he'd lost might drag him under, like getting caught in a riptide. His personal history was a churning ocean upon which he navigated. It was the engine that pushed him on, spurring him forward to achieve justice for those who had been done wrong. Trying to give a voice to those who may not have one.

He moved some of the scraps of paper around. How might they look in a different pattern? What were the consequences of putting unlikely aspects together?

There were motivations a plenty. The opportunities and means were all there too.

Stanley stroked his chin in contemplation.

All these different stories. Each being told from different perspectives. Some reliable, others not so much. All of them bubbling away in the melting pot.

He was getting philosophical.

Perhaps, he wondered, George had been on to something. An idea that real-life is all rather flimsy, and that it only exists because of the stories people tell: to each other and ourselves. And by encouraging tales to be shared, life could open up more possibilities and understanding.

Stanley sensed the swirling ocean beneath him. How different things might've been if their stories had been shared sooner.

He pulled himself back from the abyss. The painting on the wall loomed down upon him.

Keep focused, he instructed himself. The answer, he felt sure, lay before him. All it required was logic and a brave dash of lateral thinking.

Just then, he jolted. So deep in his thoughts that he hadn't seen the person arrive.

A man stood near the pond. He wore grimy jeans and a green T-shirt with a logo stitched on it, but was too distant to see what it said. His hair was grey and wiry.

The fact that Stanley hadn't noticed his arrival made him feel a touch disturbed. It brought home how vulnerable a person might be living at Riplingham Barn alone.

Suppressing his unexpected anxiety, Stanley made himself known through the windows. Drawing closer to the man it made sense.

He opened the door. 'Are you here for the oil?'

'Yes,' said the man. 'Are you Patrick?'

'No. Patrick is up at the farm. He told me to expect you.'

Stanley saw that the man's hands were stained black with grease.

'It's been a while since I've been here,' said the man. 'I'd forgotten how narrow the roads are around these parts. It made me remember how cold it was the last time I came. Must've been the middle of winter.'

Stanley thought of the scraps of paper lying on the

floor. Something niggled at him. It was the things that had been unspoken. That's what he was struggling with. The unseen links between those disparate observations.

The man went on to ask if Stanley would mind assisting him in reversing down the driveway. He'd pulled up at the top of the laneway. If Stanley could walk behind the lorry as he backed it in, he would be grateful. To this, Stanley agreed and duly directed the driver by flagging his arms as it slowly beeped backwards to the barn. Its wing mirrors brushed against the hedgerows until eventually it reached the wider opening near the pond. Stanley watched, impressed, as the driver manoeuvred the vehicle to the empty oil tank. He stood back as the man leapt from the van and skilfully attached a hosepipe contraption from the vehicle to the vessel.

The engine chugged as oil pumped into the tank. It took no more than ten minutes to fill.

On completion, the hose was detached and replaced on the lorry. The engine was turned off and the contrasting silence seemed particularly empty.

'Would you mind signing the paperwork?' he said, reaching into the cab to retrieve a clipboard from the passenger seat. 'I just need a signature to confirm delivery.'

Stanley took the board and pen. He scribbled his name where indicated.

'You said you last filled up during the winter?'

'That's right,' he said. 'Can't remember the exact date. Must've been in the new year. We was expecting snow. You wasn't here then though.'

'No. You remember?'

He looked at his boots. 'Are you a friend? Of the men who live here?'

Stanley didn't comprehend. What did he mean? The *men*?

'There was only *one* man who *lived* here?'

The driver shuffled awkwardly on the spot. Stanley sensed that the man wanted to scarper. As if he'd said the wrong thing. But Stanley kept hold of the clipboard and pen, preventing his departure.

'I don't want to cause no trouble.'

'You won't cause any trouble. But why did you say *men*?'

'I'd parked at the end of the laneway, just as I did today. When I walked down to the barn I saw them through the windows. I don't have no problem with it, but I felt a bit awkward. Like I was intruding on them.'

Stanley asked him to describe them to him. Just so that he could be sure.

The descriptions he gave were clear.

'And they were being intimate?' said Stanley.

'Yes,' said the driver. 'They were hugging and kissing. You know, in a passionate type of way. Practically ripping each other's clothes off. It looked intense. Not the type of thing I encounter much on my rounds. It's why it stuck in my memory, I suppose.'

Stanley supposed that the man was afraid that his disclosure might've caused a domestic rift, thinking that perhaps Stanley could be an injured party in an illicit affair. It made him feel even closer to George.

He handed back the clipboard and pen.

'I hope I haven't said the wrong thing,' said the man. 'I'm only telling you what I saw.'

Stanley reassured him that it was all okay. He thanked him for his honesty.

And as the lorry rumbled away, Stanley wondered at how an outsider – much like himself – had shone a light upon a dark corner of Littleworth.

CHAPTER NINETEEN

It wasn't unheard of for Ursula to take a trip to undertake research for a novel. There were often historical details that needed to be checked, or locations to be visited to ensure that the way she remembered them was accurate. She was often amazed at how unreliable her memory could be. To recall something vividly in her mind's eye, only to discover that the reality bore no resemblance to what she recalled.

So to have booked a taxi under the pretence of such a reconnaissance mission had come as no surprise to Quentin. She'd been nervous that her behaviour might've appeared different to him. Funny, she thought, how lying to someone made one self-conscious. It felt as if she'd slipped into somebody else's skin, acutely aware of the way she spoke and the manner in which she moved. What it meant that Quentin hadn't seemed to notice, she didn't know.

'I'll buy an off-peak return at Eastbourne,' she'd said.

'To London?'

'Yes.'

How she might explain in the future the obvious

absence of London in the finished draft, she wasn't sure. She would cross that bridge when she reached it. There were always ways of framing these things differently. Writing had taught her that. Never to be so strong in a belief that everything must be set in stone. She thought of the numerous drafts that her novels underwent, and how she'd learnt not to be too precious about killing her darlings, as the expression went.

The taxi dropped her at Eastbourne station where she avoided the machines, instead opting to purchase a ticket from the office. Technology was a challenge for her. George had told her that it was nothing to be afraid of. He'd said it wasn't all scary. In fact, there were many ways in which it could help her. To make her life easier. He'd even shown her his mobile phone and tablet. Yet it remained alien to her. Probably, she thought, a generational difference, or the consequence of having lived in the remote countryside for too long.

She thought of George as she clutched the ticket in her hand and made her way to the automated gates to the platforms. The overhead display boards were crammed with information, so she asked a uniformed supervisor for advice.

'London Victoria?' she said.

'Platform two, madam. It departs in five minutes.'

'Thank you.'

The train was quiet, so she was able to find a seat alone by a window. She was thankful for the opportunity to sit silently with her thoughts. In her handbag she'd brought with her an A5 lined exercise book. It was the type she preferred for jotting down ideas. An intensely private place to write freely without fear of being criticised or judged. It was in this book that she had copied down the address. Not of course from the internet, but from a page in one of the books that lived in Quentin's study. She'd checked that it was the current edition, so was confident it was up to date. She also borrowed a well-thumbed copy of the London A to Z which now nestled in her bag.

She was so caught up in her head, that she hardly noticed the train slide out of the station. Potential ways that the conversation might go played in her imagination. Having thought she'd decided how to approach it, being faced with the reality of it brought an overwhelming wave of self-doubt. It wasn't the type of thing she was used to doing, instigating difficult conversations.

Her gaze drifted out through the grimy window.

During the ninety-minute journey, she chewed anxiously on her bottom lip. The train stopped at the designated stations along the way. People embarked, and people stepped off. Each platform towards London seemed to hold more passengers. Such a contrast to Littleworth, where crowds were uncommon.

As she continued to rehearse what she might say, she began to look surreptitiously at faces on those around her. At each stop she squinted at the jostling crowds.

It had been so many years since she'd seen her. She began to wonder, with a growing feeling of panic, that perhaps she might not recognise her at all. Would she still look the same? It was unlikely. Not after all this time. In what ways might she have changed?

The feeling of being in someone else's body felt more pronounced than ever. It was a version of herself that she didn't recognise. In all their years together, she'd always stuck to her own lane, believing that her relationship with Quentin was better that way.

The carriage had transformed into a different place. How quickly, she thought, things can change. All the seats were now occupied and even the aisle between them filled up with passengers. The air was thick with sounds: muffled drumbeats, chatter, a baby crying. It was the sort of human noise that was rarely heard in the countryside. The clamour of urban living. A consequence of people living in close proximity to one another.

At London Victoria, she gathered up her bag and held back until the other people aboard had scrambled hastily for the doors. When the way looked to be a little clearer, she got to her feet. The journey hadn't resulted in her knowing exactly what she'd say, but the distance from home had bolstered her resolve. It made her almost march towards the exit barriers. She had come this far. She wouldn't turn back now.

Outside the station, she saw the black cabs lined up with their lights on but decided instead to walk. She didn't think it was far, and it would provide an opportunity to calm her nerves.

Had it always been like this? Thinking back on it now, she supposed it had. Ever since their first furtive dates at tucked away restaurants, Ursula had always been acutely aware of her relationship with Quentin's family. It had never sat comfortably with her. She'd often wondered whether, if it'd just been his wife, things might have been easier. They might've been able to cut all ties entirely and move on cleanly from his old life. It hadn't just been Nancy though. There'd been Skye to think about too. To have a child had complicated the situation.

Ursula looked at the cracks in the pavement as she strode towards her destination. What was it people said about slipping between cracks in pavements? Her mind was all over the place.

It had been like walking a tightrope, she remembered. Wanting to be with Quentin, and yet terrified at the prospect of how this brought his daughter into her life. She'd felt guilty that Skye was torn between her parents whose animosity towards one another created a tug of war for their daughter's affection. On many occasions, Ursula had wanted to speak up. To suggest other ways that the situation might be handled differently. Instead, however, adopted a passive stance. Choosing not to voice her opinion. Standing on the side-lines as a bystander.

The city clanged and hooted around her. A helicopter whirred over-head.

What a contrast George must've noticed when he'd moved to Littleworth, she thought. How quiet and sleepy it must've seemed.

It was George who'd made her wonder what Skye was doing now. Not that she hadn't thought about it before. Just that in having George to talk to she'd started to question whether things might be different.

Wasn't there – like George had attempted – always a possibility of *change*. She'd taken such great care not to overstep the mark when it had come to parenting. But with hindsight, the bond she'd forged with Skye had been a strong one. She'd taken great care not to interfere or judge. She recalled listening to Skye's perspectives. Looking on proudly as she grew into a strong-minded young woman, which having such headstrong parents came as no surprise.

And yet, there was always the kernel of guilt on Ursula's behalf that the rift between Skye's parents was of her doing. Would Skye's upbringing have been more settled if her parents had stayed together acrimoniously?

There was no answer to that. The clocks could not be turned back.

It was just in talking to George – sharing her story – that she'd come to wonder if things could be different now. She thought depressingly of the birthday cards sent to her. All of them representing a year that had been missed. Time that might've been spent with the daughter she'd never had. Did that have to mean that a bridge couldn't still be built? Isn't there always a chance to fix things that went wrong?

'To give up hope is to give up on life,' George had said.

That's what had really spurred her on. She hadn't given up on life. She couldn't believe that. And so it followed that she hadn't given up on hope...

It was that which had brought her to the steps before her. She looked up at the door and the little polished

166

brass plaque beside it. To see the name made it real. It was what George had encouraged her to do.

'Just be brave,' he'd said. 'What's the worst that can happen?'

And with that, she took a step up and steadied herself for she was about to face…

CHAPTER TWENTY

Stanley spent some time contemplating the description given by the oil delivery driver. He could think of no reason why the man's account shouldn't be accurate. Impossible, actually, for him to have described George and his companion that day in such detail. He hadn't considered it before, and he wondered why.

He stood in the very spot where the men had embraced, not realising at first that they'd been on full display through the vast windows. Lost, for that moment, in each other's company.

Risky, thought Stanley. Anyone could've seen them. But from what he knew of George, perhaps there lay a thrill there? A frisson of excitement in the potential danger of being caught. George, from what he understood, had enjoyed living on the edge.

It certainly muddied the waters.

Yet through what circumstances this liaison had come about, Stanley didn't know. He had some theories, though. He weighed them up as he looked again at his copious notes. The scraps of paper were now arranged in chronological order. A potential timeline of events began to emerge. A sequence of cause and effect. Maybe a deadly game of consequences.

The situation required answers, but Stanley was sensitive to the potential ramifications. He would try and handle it discreetly. The phone number was easy enough to look up online, and he was just punching the numbers into his mobile when Bridget arrived.

He was half expecting her.

She approached the barn with a frown. Her cheeks looked red.

Conscious of his scribblings laid out upon the floor, Stanley stepped outside to intercept her.

'Why didn't you tell me?' she said. 'You should've warned me that you were going to speak to Joyce.'

'Warned you?'

'Oh, that's probably not the right expression. I mean, you should've given me a heads up. So that I could've prepared myself. You know, as to what I was going to say.'

Stanley wasn't sure he comprehended. She was in danger of tying herself up in knots.

'I thought you didn't want people to know you're a private investigator?' she said. 'You said you were going to keep that under wraps. Do things undercover.'

'Things have changed. The situation has progressed. I changed my mind.'

'Changed? Progressed? In what ways?'

'More details have come into my possession. Further information that made it too difficult to continue concealing my profession.' He watched for any shift in demeanour that might shed further light on the investigation, but she retained the disgruntled look upon her face. 'I wanted to hear Joyce's version of events. To hear what she had to say.'

'I don't see what Joyce has to do with anything. She barely spoke to George.'

'Did Joyce tell you what we discussed?'

'I haven't spoken to her about it. Not yet, anyway.'

Stanley was curious. 'Then how do you know I met with her?'

'She spoke to Patrick. Told him that you're a private investigator. Said you'd been asking questions about the night before George was found.' She folded her arms. 'He demanded to know whether I already knew, about why you were here. It put me in a difficult situation.'

'Did you tell him that you knew?'

She looked indignant. 'Yes. I told him that I didn't want to upset everything again. That's why I'd kept it to myself. He's not happy. He thought it was all over with the outcome of the inquest. He's worried that this story is *never* going to go away.'

Stanley wished he could give a reassurance.

'I'm sorry that it's made things difficult for you,' he said. 'But I have to do my job.'

Bridget turned her face away from him as if unable to look him in the eye. He saw tears well up as she stared at the walled kitchen and where the storytelling huts should now have stood. She was thinking again, he guessed, of her brother.

170

'Imogen knows too,' he said, 'that I'm a private investigator.'

'She does?'

'Yes. She overheard my conversation with Joyce. She told me that she'd listened to what we'd talked about.'

Her focus withdrew from the garden vista and focused back on Stanley. 'What exactly did you talk to Joyce about? That's what I'd like to know.'

Stanley gave an honest description of their interaction in the farmhouse kitchen. His account of George slipping away from The Plough that evening to confront Joyce on her behaviour towards her daughter-in-law threatened to make her welling tears overflow.

'That sounds like George,' she sniffed. 'Deep down he believed in protecting those closest to him. He didn't always know how to show it, or express it, but he loved us. Those of us nearest to him, I mean.'

Stanley believed it. He had done for some time now.

'I think your brother had a good heart,' he said.

This appeared to appease her a little. Her arms, still wrapped around herself, loosened a little. She looked exhausted. 'Nobody wants to be thought of in a bad light,' she said. 'Especially when it's not justified.'

It was the opening he'd been hoping for. The opportunity to hear her side of the story.

'Joyce said that George had accused her of treating you badly when you'd moved to Downlands Farm. Said that she'd seen Patrick as the blue-eyed boy. I don't know why – yet I have an idea – but I think she gave an edited version of that conversation. Would you agree?'

171

'Yes,' she said. 'It wouldn't have been like George to have held back.' She suddenly flung her head back and looked up to the clouds. She gave an exasperated cry.

'Are you okay?'

'Oh, it's all such a mess. Looking back, it's all just *such* a mess.'

He gave her a moment to regain her composure. Then said, 'Did you know that George confronted Joyce?'

'I suspected,' she replied. 'I noticed that something had changed in her behaviour towards me. There was a shift in her attitude. I put it down to her being sympathetic. Going softer on me because of George dying. She hadn't long lost her husband. I thought that might've been it. Then part of me wondered whether George had said something, but I couldn't think when that might've happened.'

Stanley cast his mind back to his initial research. 'I found an article about you online,' he said.

She looked unsurprised. 'I thought you'd find that. It doesn't take a genius to type into a search engine.'

'So why didn't you say anything?'

'It's not easy to talk about. I try to pretend that it never happened. That it might just vanish. That somehow history might re-write itself.'

'Even so, you confided in George?' said Stanley. 'You talked to him about it.'

'That's right. I wanted him to know the truth. He was a good listener. One of George's strengths was his ability not to judge. That's a special quality in a person.'

Stanley liked to think that such qualities could be attributed to him. However challenging a case may be, he always strived to treat those involved as human beings. Sensitive to the light and shade that lies in everyone.

'I suppose Joyce knew of the story?' he asked.

'Patrick told her that there would be a story in the news. We thought it best to warn her. I suppose she formed an opinion on what she read. It didn't cast me in a favourable light.'

The headline shone in Stanley's mind eye. It had been damning. He could see how Joyce might've drawn her conclusions.

'There was more to it, wasn't there,' said Stanley. 'The headline and report didn't represent the truth.'

'No,' she said. 'You're right. It didn't.'

It came as no surprise to him. He rarely accepted things on face value with no supporting evidence. His own experience had taught him that.

'The report said that you'd been found in possession of cocaine,' he said. 'That you'd picked it up innocently in a bathroom toilet. That wasn't what happened, was it?'

'I'd had an inkling that things weren't going well. I saw that Patrick was on edge. I'd encouraged him to branch out on his own, so I wasn't sure what to do when the business didn't take off.'

Stanley rewound his memory to his conversation with Patrick. 'He told me that he left a job as chef to open a restaurant.'

'I had my doubts at first. I worried that it was a bit of

a gamble, putting all our eggs in one basket.'

'Is that what you did?'

'Financially, yes. And I suppose emotionally too. Patrick had always struggled with his career. We thought that him being his own boss would be good for him. I just think we underestimated how much an enterprise like that hangs on the shoulders of one person.'

'It sounds like he was under a lot of pressure.'

'He was. The restaurant wasn't bringing in enough to cover the bills. We had borrowed against our own home, so I think he felt the pressure of that too. I don't think he's the first one to try and find a way to cope.'

'The cocaine?'

'I knew Patrick had dabbled with cannabis. A joint at the end of a shift in the hotel kitchen. It was something I just turned a blind eye too. But cocaine was something else. He said it was just to try and keep him going. He was burning the candle at both ends. I didn't like it.'

Stanley guessed the rest.

'On that night out, when the drugs were found in your bag, why didn't you tell the police that they belonged to Patrick?'

'I had to make a snap decision. All I could think of was the mountain of debt. I wondered what damage a story like that might do to the already failing restaurant. I didn't want to admit Patrick had a problem with drugs. I wanted to protect him. I couldn't throw him under the bus.'

The choice she'd made in that moment had cost her

174

the career she loved. She'd sacrificed her identity for the love of her husband.

She continued: 'The tragedy of it all, of course, was that my choice meant nothing in the end. Because when the pandemic hit the restaurant was doomed anyway. Not only did I lose my job, but we ended up losing the business as well.'

'And you told George all this?'

'Yes,' she said.

'I can see why he might feel aggrieved at Joyce's treatment of you if she wrongly believed you were the guilty party. It must have riled him to see Patrick being treated favourably when the responsibility lay with him.'

'I tried to tell George that it wasn't black and white. There was nobody to blame. Patrick had been struggling and was trying to cope in whatever way he could. I should have been more careful. I only did what I thought was right.'

Stanley churned over the events in his mind. He tried to imagine how Joyce might've reacted to hearing the truth about Patrick, and he wondered why she hadn't told him. Could she have been angry at being told the whole story? It brought him back again to possible motives. Emotions that may have boiled over.

'Maybe if you spoke to Patrick,' she said, 'he might understand. It might make him see that you're trying to do the best thing for George. Would you mind?'

'No. I wouldn't. I'll do my best to put his mind at rest.'

She thanked him. 'If we go now, we might catch him

heading out to the paddock…'

Stanley apologised. He wouldn't be able to speak to him immediately. It would have to wait. There was something pressing that he must attend to first. He saw that she was disappointed. She'd hoped he'd accompany her back to Downlands Farm. Perhaps, he thought, she hadn't wanted to face it alone.

But Stanley was thinking of the number he'd begun to dial on his phone. He sensed it was important. So he would make that call first, before doing anything else. Just to be sure.

CHAPTER TWENTY-ONE

The water was still. Insects hopped across it, creating tiny circles amongst the lily pads, barely visible to the naked eye. Stanley contemplated his own shadow outlined on the pond. The black shape rippled.

It was the very spot that George had either tripped or been pushed. Easy to see, in both scenarios, how hitting his head on one of those rocks could've knocked him out cold before drowning in the icy water.

Stanley worried that time was no longer on his side. Now that his reason for coming to Littleworth was being shared amongst the locals, he feared that his chances of getting them to open up to him would dwindle. They would be suspicious of him now.

He heard someone approach. Shoes crunched towards him on the ground. Not like on the night it happened, Stanley thought. On that occasion, the blanket of snow would've hidden the sound. George wouldn't have heard a thing.

Stanley turned. It was who he expected.

'What's this all about?' they said.

He looked different. It was seeing him outside and in

a different environment. Stanley hadn't noticed before how tall and strapping he was. Bearing in mind his previous career, it was understandable.

'Thanks for coming to see me,' said Stanley.

'I don't appreciate being summoned. Especially when we're trying to cope with the lunch trade. Zara needs all the help she can get in her condition.'

Will Solomon's body language was assertive. To possess a natural air of authority, Stanley thought, would be useful as a landlord. A physical presence to allay any rowdy behaviour. No doubt he would've made a fierce opponent on the rugby pitch.

'I thought it best to talk discreetly,' said Stanley. 'For your sake.'

'What do you mean? You said on the phone that you're a private investigator. Which didn't surprise me.'

'No?'

'I didn't believe for a second that you were just a tourist. Not after all those questions you were asking. I thought you were just another journalist sniffing around. Looking for gossip.'

Stanley shook his head. 'Perhaps I should've been upfront with you.'

'Well, you can be upfront with me now. What is it you're investigating? Is it to do with Zara's father?' Stanley thought of the scandal surrounding Hector Lyons. It clearly still cast a long shadow over their lives. Perhaps it would never go away. Something to learn to live with. A constant burden to always be carried around. 'Or is it to do with what happened to

George? Here at Riplingham Barn. You asked a lot of questions about that.'

Stanley bided his time. A pregnant pause. A moment to evaluate Will's face before he dropped the revelation. Waiting just enough to see him squirm.

'Did you know that you'd been seen?' asked Stanley.

'Seen?' said Will. 'What do you mean? Seen? Where?'

Stanley didn't say a word. He simply moved his eyes. To the very place that the oil delivery driver had said.

Then looked back to witness his reaction.

Will opened his mouth as if to speak, but no words came out. He gawped. He looked to be floundering. Like a fish taken out of the pond.

All of a sudden, his physical strength seemed somehow to drift away. Replaced, instead, with a vulnerable expression on his face.

'You and George Thorpe were in a relationship?' asked Stanley.

'What's this all about?' said Will again. 'Have you been spying on me?'

It wasn't illogical that Will had jumped to the wrong conclusion. It was true that the job of a private investigator often involved proving indiscretions. Gathering evidence for divorce cases or the custody of children.

'I'm investigating the events surrounding George's death. My focus is on whether it was an accident or not. So, it's about him, not you.'

'But the inquest?'

'Sometimes mistakes happen.' Stanley said, speaking from the heart. 'I'm not here to judge. I just want to

179

establish the facts. To make sure that the correct outcome was reached.'

Will dug his hands in his trouser pockets. He looked like he'd been summoned to the headteacher's office. He hung his head and pushed the toe of his shoe into the ground. Was he sulking?

'I suppose it doesn't look very good, does it? Us skulking around in the shadows like that.'

'I'm not here to judge. I just want to gather the facts. To potentially rule you out of the investigation.'

Stanley was prepared to take his time. It looked as if Will was gathering his thoughts. Was the story more complex than he'd assumed? Or perhaps the tale was longer than he'd anticipated? 'Can you tell me how it came about? Your relationship with George?'

'It wasn't what I'd describe as a relationship. It was more of a fling, I suppose. Or to be more specific, an old flame.'

'An old flame? You knew George before he moved to Littleworth?' It wasn't what Stanley was expecting, but it began to make sense.

'We were very young. Both free and single. That time in life when you don't realise how carefree you are. Unrestrained by future responsibilities and the trappings of being a grown-up. I'd never met anyone as confident in their own skin. George was entirely comfortable with his sexuality. He knew who he was. He didn't care what anybody thought of him.'

'Did that make him attractive to you?'

'Well they say opposites attract, don't they? I was questioning my sexuality at the time. I was trying to find my way. It was as if there were different routes ahead of me. Different directions being pointed to on a sign-post. George said he'd remembered that summer together in our youth as if it had a golden haze. He described me as his first true love. I can't say that's how I felt, but I was fond of him. I just knew deep down that at the time I couldn't see how our being together could work.'

'Why was that?' Stanley asked.

'Maybe times were different then. I felt forced into choosing one way or another. I was worried about what impact a label might have on me. It's so long ago. I can't really explain it very well now. I remember worrying what other people would think. Not sure what the consequences might be.'

'You were afraid of being judged?'

'Whilst I may have been George's first love, he wasn't mine. My passion was rugby. It was the only thing I wanted to do in life. It was everything to me. My identity. I couldn't believe that a professional rugby career was feasible if I was with a man. So I was faced with a stark choice. To go one way or another.'

'And you chose rugby.'

'I'd spent my entire life training towards a professional playing career. So when the opportunity arrived, I couldn't face turning it down. There was expectation from my family and friends. They all knew how much I wanted it too.'

Stanley wasn't one to believe that life had to be lived rigidly. He sympathised with the situation Will had found himself in. Identities and dreams can be fluid.

Things can shift and change based on circumstance. The various seasons of life, he had concluded, could see a person playing very different roles.

'I hadn't thought of it as any more than a young summer fling. The two of us sort of playing around.'

'But you say George thought more of it than that?'

'He said he'd always had me at the back of his mind. Silently holding a candle for me. He told me that he would never have done anything about it if his partner hadn't died. When Simeon died he was suddenly all alone. He said he couldn't help wondering what had come of me. Whether things could've been different between us if we'd met at a different time. I suppose he thought of me as the one who'd got away.

'It hadn't been difficult for him to track me down online,' he continued. 'Everything's on social media these days, isn't it? It sounds unlikely, but that's why he moved to Littleworth. He thought the fact that Riplingham Barn was for sale, right on my doorstep, was a sign. He wanted to make a clean break from London. He thought it was fate. It was the sort of grand gesture that George made. He wasn't one to be limited by rules. He liked to live his life *hopefully*.'

It sounded intense. But George, surely, wasn't the first one to have been driven by first love. To never have accepted that there might still be something in it.

'When did you come to realise that George had become your neighbour?'

'I remember it vividly. It was the first winter we'd owned the pub. A bitterly cold day. Trade was much slower than we'd hoped. We made the decision to close our doors during the afternoons as there were no customers at that time. I would go for a run each day, to try and clear my thoughts. It was habit from the past and important to keep my strength up after the injury I'd had. I must've pushed myself hard that day as I was practically bent double outside the pub, out of breath. It was there I saw somebody finishing a conversation with Doug, the farmer, at the gates of Downlands Farm. The pair of them went their separate ways, with the stranger walking up towards me. I didn't recognise him at first. Why would I? Not after all that time. He was wrapped up in a thick coat, scarf and hat. He hadn't looked well. He had a terrible cough. It was only as he got close and said my name that I realised who he was.

'He told me that he'd been introducing himself to the locals. He was full of cold. Spluttering and wheezing. Later he'd said that it wasn't how he'd hoped I'd see him again for the first time. It was hardly the romantic reunion scene he'd imagined.'

Stanley mentally added this account to the chronologically ordered scraps of paper laid out on the floor. He wondered whether George had aggressively pursued his old flame, and if doing so in the knowledge of his marriage to Zara whether it meant a re-evaluation of George's moral compass. It raised questions of Will too.

'It takes two to tango,' said Will, as if reading Stanley's mind. 'I don't condone it. We just got caught up in it all. In each other and the memories. It wasn't long after George had moved here that the country went into lockdown. We struck up a friendship again. We walked together over the downs. We reminisced about that golden summer when everything had seemed both possible and inevitably doomed.'

'Did you continue to see each other after the lockdowns lifted?'

'After the initial rekindling, we settled into almost a sort of unspoken arrangement. George wasn't pressuring me to make any changes. It was more of a friendship with benefits, you might say. He was encouraging me with developing trade at the pub, and I was supporting him with his storytelling huts.'

'Until something changed?'

'Yes,' said Will. 'When Zara told me she was pregnant. It shook me out of myself. Made me think about what I really wanted. And what was *right*. I felt guilty about how we'd been sneaking about. It was the moment we were seen by that delivery driver that I really panicked. It brought home how risky what we were doing was.'

'So you told George it was over?'

'I did. He said it felt like history repeating itself. That I'd led him up the garden path. Which I didn't think was very fair. Although, he had a point.'

'He didn't take it very well then?'

Will shook his head. 'I suppose you're pinning motives on me now? Are you wondering whether I could kill him to stop him telling Zara? Or are you wondering whether she knew, and lashed out at him in anger?'

'Did she know?'

He looked into the pond. 'Honestly, I don't know. If she does, she's never said.'

There were certainly potential motives, but Stanley had a hunch that these might only distract from the other theories he'd been building.

'That evening at The Plough,' said Stanley, 'the one before George was discovered dead. Can you give me your perspective?'

'I was nervous about it. I was worried that George had an ulterior motive for gathering everyone in the pub. Not just for Imogen's birthday. I was worried that he might stand up and tell everyone what we'd been up to in secret. Which is probably unfair, as George wasn't like that as a person. It's just that he'd seemed erratic leading up to that night. And that evening he was drinking heavily which only increased my concern that he might do something silly.'

'Did you speak to him at all that evening?'

'He followed me into the toilets. He was sort of talking to himself, babbling stuff that sounded like nonsense.'

'What was he saying?'

'Most of it was incoherent. His speech was slurred. He was muttering something about him being in possible danger. That they wouldn't like it. The only thing I remember him saying clearly was "*I've told her now*". I took him by the shoulders and shook him. I asked him whether he meant Zara? Had he told Zara about us? But he said how could I think that of him. He said that he would never do that to me. He said he guessed I didn't really know him at all. And I remember being confused. If not Zara, then who? Told who? About what?'

'What did he say?'

'He didn't. He flung my hands off him and went back to the others.'

Whilst Will may have been confused, it all fitted exactly with Stanley's notion of events. The theories had crystallised into two distinct hypotheses. Of all the names he'd initially listed in his notebook, only two of them remained. Two individuals with the strongest of motives.

The two paths stretched out before him.

'This is important,' said Stanley, 'so think very carefully.'

'Yes?' said Will uncertainly.

'When you confronted George in the toilets? Was that before or after Imogen had blown out the candles on her birthday cake?'

Will didn't look to understand. It held no obvious significance to him. But the whole case rested on this. 'I know the answer to that. I can tell you exactly.'

And in doing so, Stanley Messina's timeline was complete. A muddle no more.

Yet if – as he was confident – he was right, the way ahead looked as treacherous and black as it had ever been.

CHAPTER TWENTY-TWO

Stanley turned the key in the lock. The exterior face of the barn loomed down upon him. If only it could speak, he thought. It might've told him earlier who had shoved George into the pond that night. For he was under no illusion now. Somebody *had* pushed him into that icy water. It had been no accident. The act had been carried out with intent and with strong motive.

He looked once more at the immediate surrounds of Riplingham Barn. The late afternoon sun lit up the overgrown plants within the kitchen garden. It shone a mellow gold. An almost imperceptible haze lingered over the mirrored surface of the pond.

Had there been a chance that George might've lived happily ever after here? His now known pursuit of a young love may not have been successful, but that didn't mean he couldn't have moved on from it. He had been clutching at straws. Some might've accused him of betraying Simeon Dean. To try and move on so quickly. But grief manifests in strange forms. Stanley wondered whether George had feared being on his own after Simeon's death. George, he reasoned, had simply been trying to find his way.

No crime in that.

He looked again at the painting on the wall before setting off purposefully along the laneway. Having examined the various tangled threads of his investigation, the time had come to tie the ends together as neatly as possible.

Having spoken to Will, he looked at The Plough through new eyes. The floral window boxes looked so garish today, he wondered whether perhaps they might be artificial. Perhaps, like the repurposed telephone box, its exterior belied the truth within. The same, he thought, could be applied to Flint Cottage. It's picket fence and climbing rose looked that afternoon particularly pretty.

He saw the tiny hamlet of Littleworth as if a film-set. The stage was set, and the players were about to reach their final act. As he passed the rusty entrance gates of Downlands Farm, he remembered what Will had said. He had suspected as much. It was all a matter of seeing things from the right angle.

Up ahead, one of the people he'd come to see was sweeping the ground outside the farmhouse with a broom. But before he'd got close enough to make himself known, a voice called out to him from the distance.

'Hey!' It was Patrick, striding quickly towards him. 'I want words with you!'

On hearing the voice, Joyce's broom froze in mid-air. She looked at the men as if a storm were approaching.

'What's all this business of yours, sneaking around poking your nose into our lives?' said Patrick as he drew near. 'You shouldn't have ambushed my mother with all your questions.'

Joyce remained silent.

The three of them stood in a triangle, not far from Jimbo's campervan.

Before Stanley had a chance to justify his actions, another person arrived. She must've heard Patrick's raised voice.

'If anyone's to blame for that,' said Bridget, 'it's me. I should've insisted that Stanley was upfront with everyone about why he was in Littleworth when he first told me.'

'I put you in that position,' said Stanley. 'So the blame lies with me. I only hope you might concede that without such methods, my investigation may not have reached the truth.'

Patrick's mood didn't seem to lighten. He seemed to be looking to Bridget and assessing whether he should continue with his complaint. 'It looks like you've played us all off against one another. Taking us for fools.'

'That wasn't my intention. I don't believe any of you are fools. I have taken this case very seriously.'

'Then why tell Bridget you're a private investigator but not tell anyone else?'

'Because I believed, and still do, that in this instance my best chance at success was to link with the person who loved George the most. The person who'd rather see justice prevail than sweep everything under the carpet.'

'He's right,' said Bridget. 'When the inquest outcome

was published, you all just wanted it to go away. If there was any doubt in my mind that George hadn't had an accident, none of you wanted me to voice it. You'd all had enough of it.'

'Oh, Bridget,' Patrick sighed. 'I never wanted you to forget George. I said as much to you. It was just that I couldn't bear to see you stuck in that loop. Re-living what had happened over and over again.'

They looked at one another searchingly. Then she addressed Stanley:

'Have I helped you at all? I can't see that I've been of much use to you.'

'On the contrary,' Stanley replied. 'You enabled me to make in-roads where it would've been difficult. You provided cover for me, helping me to fly under the radar. Just as we'd discussed. You filled me in with the backstory. And most importantly, you helped me to see George in the way you did. As the brother who meant so much to you.'

Patrick appeared to have backed off a little. He still looked affronted. 'That's all well and good,' he said, 'but has it actually proved anything different? Have you come to any other conclusion?'

'Yes,' said Stanley. 'I have.'

He let it hang in the air for a moment. To give them the chance to appreciate the gravity of his words.

'You think George was killed?' said Bridget, almost in a whisper.

'I had narrowed everything down to two people who had strong motives, although I couldn't be sure which of them was responsible. Not until I understood the order in which things had happened.'

'*Two* people?' said Bridget. '*Two* people had a strong enough reason to want George *dead*?'

Stanley knew it wouldn't be easy. No way of sugar coating it. 'One of those people was you, Joyce.'

The old woman clutched the handle of her broom.

'Joyce?' said Bridget. 'She hardly knew George.'

'This is absurd,' Patrick interjected.

'Not when the facts are established and examined,' Stanley explained. He spoke to Joyce directly, who had not moved a muscle: 'I already knew that George had come to see you that evening. Slipping away from The Plough to confront you on how you'd treated his sister. That accusation alone may have been enough to rile you. It hardly looked like a strong enough motive to kill, though. And yet, when I questioned you about that evening, you didn't tell me the entire story, did you? You told me that George had said Doug would've been ashamed of you. And you'd said he couldn't speak on behalf of someone he'd never met. But that wasn't the whole story, was it? For George *had* met Doug. And he told you so.'

Joyce's silence said it all.

'That doesn't make sense,' said Patrick. 'It doesn't add up. George didn't move to Littleworth before Dad died.'

'No,' said Stanley. 'But nobody just buys a home without viewing it first. Not without walking around the local area. Getting a feel for the surrounds, and the neighbours.' He was thinking of Will's account. His surprise at encountering George Thorpe after all those years.

It was then Joyce spoke. Her voice sounded thin in the open air. 'I'd thought about it a lot. It had never seemed possible, seeing as how we never had any visitors to Downlands Farm. You know how quiet it is here during the winter.'

'You wondered how he'd contracted the virus that killed him,' said Stanley.

'It was before we knew all about it. In the early days before we'd heard all the new terminology on the news. We didn't really believe any of it then, did we? None of us had received a vaccine. Doug had never said he'd met George. It was probably so brief that he hadn't thought it worth mentioning. He hadn't known who he was, I suppose. Just a potential purchaser for Riplingham Barn.'

'So when George told you he'd met Doug, you put the pieces together. You realised that he was the only outsider Doug had been near before he fell ill.'

She looked imploringly between her son and daughter-in-law. 'I admit that when George died, I couldn't help but feel that perhaps it was karma. It was a nasty thought, I know. Doug was my world.'

'But George couldn't have known he had the virus,' said Bridget. 'It wasn't like he gave it to Doug on purpose.'

'Of course I can see that now. It was just in the heat of the moment I blamed him. I was only focused on what I'd lost. I'm ashamed of those feelings now.'

'Is that why you didn't tell me the whole story?' asked Stanley.

'I'm not proud of feeling so angry. I'm ashamed that I wished him harm. It was almost as if I'd put a curse on him. I worried that my thoughts had brought about his death.'

'People have committed crimes for lesser motives than this,' said Stanley.

'I didn't do anything to him. You have to believe me,' she said. 'You think I crept out that night and caused him harm?'

'It would've been entirely possible. You had a motive. And the means were not beyond your capability. I might've pursued it had it not been for the birthday cake…'

'The birthday cake?' said Bridget. 'What does that have to do with anything?'

Before he had the opportunity to elaborate, Imogen emerged ethereally from the farmhouse. Stanley wondered how much of this conversation she'd overheard. He knew how much she liked to listen. It was the trait of a potential writer. To always be taking in what's going on. Observing everything acutely. Always hunting for material to build another story.

It was time now to confirm the significance of the birthday.

With Imogen now present, Stanley was in position to ask her the questions he'd prepared. He doubted that she'd realise the significance of them. Not aware of how important her recollections might be.

All eyes were upon her as she answered.

It was just as Stanley had feared.

With everyone's attention focused absolutely in

Imogen's direction, it was – however – only Stanley, having got a hunch, who noticed that the door to the campervan had slowly opened. The bearded man was stepping out into the light. He took in every word. Until he was ready to speak.

CHAPTER TWENTY-THREE

Ursula hadn't written a word all afternoon. She couldn't focus. The page remained blank before her. Her attention drawn to more serious matters.

It wasn't like her. Usually so regimented in writing her daily word count. Never in her career had she sat waiting for the elusive muse to arrive. That was the way of amateurs. No, to have written all those books upon the bookshelf required self-discipline. Getting ideas down on paper. Pushing on, even when she didn't feel inclined to do it.

But not today.

She looked, as she'd done so many times before, at the birthday cards from Skye pinned to her noticeboard. She thought again of each year they represented. How sad they looked with their curling corners.

Where should she begin?

That was often the most important thing in telling a story. Finding the right place to start. Then laying out each step of the tale in such a way that it made sense.

She heard his key in the front door, returned from his afternoon walk. As regular as clockwork.

'Shall I put the kettle on?' Quentin called up to her.

'Yes please,' she said. 'I'll come down.'

She laid her unused pen down on the pad. No words for him to type up today.

'Quite a little get together there seemed to be outside the farmhouse,' said Quentin above the bubbling water, as Ursula entered the kitchen. 'Looked like the whole family and that Stanley you had for afternoon tea.'

She recalled that afternoon with him. That's what had really got her thinking on it again.

'Is everything alright, Ursula?' he asked. 'You don't look quite yourself.'

That was just it. She didn't feel herself. Not able to shake the feeling again that she was in somebody else's skin.

'It's probably the heat,' he said. 'Go and sit yourself down. I'll bring your tea to you. Unless you'd prefer a cold drink?'

She wanted neither, but said, 'Tea. Thank you.'

As she sat waiting in the sitting room, she took in her surroundings. The trappings of their cosy existence leapt out at her. Everything from the curtains, to the furniture and the pictures had a haze of artifice about them. Extraordinary, she thought, how one can become blind to one's own habitat. How easy to take it all for granted. Until a moment like this comes along to open your eyes. A moment on which the entire future hangs.

'Ursula?' Quentin said, holding her cup out for her. 'You looked like you were lost in your thoughts. Is it the writing? Have you reached a tricky aspect of the plot?'

'Oh no,' she said, softly. She took the cup from him. 'It's not the writing.'

If only it were, she thought. She'd have been able to switch things about. Go back through her manuscript and alter the way things had happened.

'Then what is it? Tell me what's troubling you.'

Her hand began to tremble. Her cup, and the tea inside it, wobbled. She placed it down for fear of spilling it.

Where, she asked herself, was the best place to start?

'I didn't want to believe it,' she commenced. 'I *couldn't* believe it. Because, of course, if I did believe it, then everything else I've ever known would be a lie.'

Quentin laughed. 'That's a jolly good riddle. You're going to have to say more if I'm going to be able to help you with it.'

She didn't like his laughter.

'It was Stanley that got me thinking about it all again, I suppose. As I said, I hadn't *wanted* to believe it. Not the first time. Not when George suggested it.'

'George?'

'It wasn't exactly the same. But they both said that the dead deserve justice. For the truth to be told.'

Quentin's face had changed. The laughter had gone from his eyes. 'You've lost me I'm afraid. I don't know what you're saying.'

Ursula straightened the hem on her skirt with her trembling fingers. 'But you do, Quentin. Don't you.'

She had started the story at the wrong point. It was

197

the wrong place in time entirely.

She would try again.

'After you left Nancy for me, Skye was caught between you both. As a teenager, she was like a pawn in a game. Each of you vying for her undivided attention. Trying to turn her against the other.' She spoke as if to herself. Telling herself the tale. 'I think, perhaps, as Skye spent the majority of time with her mother, you had the upper hand. You didn't have to play the role of disciplinarian. Never had to take on the daily responsibilities of her growing up. Instead, drifting in and out of her life at whim.

'During her final year at school, she applied to study Law at university. I recall some vague disagreement about this between you and Nancy. You were in favour of the idea, feeling that it would be a sensible career path. Nancy had concerns that Skye was neglecting her other creative interests.

'When Skye received her A Level results, she decided to defer her university place and take a gap year. Whilst you were reticent, you reluctantly agreed that it would give her time to be confident she was taking the right career path.'

Ursula looked to Quentin for confirmation that this is how it had been. He'd lowered his eyes, absorbed in studying the frayed carpet.

'On leaving school,' Ursula continued, 'the dynamic between the three of you changed. Skye began to find her independence at home, which caused friction between her and Nancy. No longer was she prepared to stick by the rules imposed by her mother. They had a falling out over Skye staying out late or hanging out with boys. Something blown out of all proportion. So Skye packed a bag and came to stay here.

'It put me in a tricky spot. Flint Cottage is small. But we made space for her. I think it was difficult for you too. Not so easy to be the favourite parent when there is no handing back of your child at the end of the day. Maybe she was under some kind of illusion that we lived an exciting life. Different from that of her upbringing with her mother.'

Her story began to ramble. It wouldn't do. She needed to bring it back to the crux of it all.

'It was a day in the autumn. I remember the sun being lower in the sky. The trees were changing colour. Skye announced that she had met a boy and was going to go travelling. She didn't know where they were going or for how long.' Ursula addressed Quentin directly: 'You didn't react well to this. Did you?'

'Of course I didn't. I hadn't got a clue who she was going off with. It was ridiculous.'

'I think there was more to it than that. You saw your own self reflected in her. It reminded you of how you'd abandoned your own studies when you'd met Nancy at a party. Your reaction was so out of proportion. I think it shocked Skye.'

The room had grown airless. Its heat pressed upon Ursula.

'She had a bag. I remember it being tugged between you both as you argued in the hallway. She wrenched it away from you and made her way up the garden path. She said she was walking to the station where the boy would meet her. I watched from the window as you pursued her until you were both out of sight. You'd headed down the path that's overgrown now.'

Ursula took a breath.

'You were gone such a long time,' she said. 'I remember the light fading. When, eventually, you came back your face was white. I asked you what had happened. And you'd said that she wouldn't listen. That you couldn't make her see sense.'

'She wouldn't listen,' said Quentin quietly. 'She really wouldn't listen to me.'

'You told me that she'd said she hadn't wanted anything to do with you or Nancy.'

'I could see how much it had upset you,' said Quentin. 'You were so worried about her. I knew that you were hoping that she might return for Christmas.'

It was true.

'I didn't hear from her until the new year,' said Ursula, 'when I received a birthday card from her. That first card had a brief line telling me not to worry about her. She said she'd gone back to her mother's house and still intended to go travelling. It was post marked London. I felt such relief in knowing that she was safe. It made me hopeful that one day things might repair themselves. Perhaps that's why I didn't see. I *wanted* to believe it.'

She thought of her recent trip to the capital. How much courage she'd needed to go and see Nancy. To visit the offices of that publishing house. To face her demons after all those years. To learn that Nancy had been lied to as well.

Her story had dove-tailed back to her previous words. 'It was George who tried to tell me. Having shown him the birthday cards, he tried to find out where Skye was now. But he couldn't find a record of her anywhere. There were no details of her having had a job. No trace of her having got married. It was as if she'd completely vanished. He told me too that you'd lashed out at Imogen during her work experience with us. I hadn't known about that. You hadn't told me. She said she'd been unwell. Of course, I don't believe that now.

'In the end, it was the story-telling huts that made me really wonder. I thought you'd been opposed to them because you'd feared they'd bring outsiders to Littleworth. Ruin the peace and quiet. But that wasn't it at all, was it?'

Quentin said nothing.

'It was because of where they'd be built,' she said, hardly daring to believe the words forming in her mouth. 'Because that's where she is. Isn't she?'

She wasn't sure how he'd react. She thought there might be a denial. He placed his hands on his knees and grabbed hard until his knuckles were white. He began to shake his head. He shot to his feet.

'She wouldn't listen to me,' he said, manically stomping on the spot. 'She was making such a big mistake. Throwing away her opportunities. Too young to understand the consequences. I begged her to come back to Flint Cottage, so we could talk about it rationally. One moment I was tugging at her arm, the next – in the tussle – she'd lost her footing. She slipped

201

and hit her head on one of the tree roots. She wasn't moving. I checked to see if she was breathing. But she wasn't.'

'Why didn't you get help?'

'I panicked.'

Worried, she supposed, about what others would think of him.

'I tried to revive her, but it didn't work. She was gone. So I dragged her into the undergrowth until later when I…'

Ursula couldn't bear to hear the words. An image of him with a shovel reared up in her imagination.

'How could you let me go on thinking for all these years that she was okay, when all the time she was out there?'

Ursula too got to her feet. She wasn't sure she could bear being in the same room as him.

'I saw how happy it made you to receive a birthday card from her. Once I'd sent one, it just sort of made sense to send the others.'

She wasn't sure how he'd done it. To have them sent from different locations. She wasn't sure of anything now.

'It was an accident,' he pleaded. 'You have to believe me.'

Ursula backed out of the room to the hallway, but Quentin followed.

'And George?' she croaked. 'Was he an accident too?'

'He wouldn't give up,' said Quentin. 'He was determined to build those storytelling huts. And I knew, if he did, they'd find the body. You'd know immediately that I'd been lying to you and you'd put the pieces together. Can't you see? I *had* to stop him.'

Her back was now against the front door. She didn't want to be near him.

'Get away from me,' she said, scrambling for the door handle behind her. 'Get away from me!'

But he came for her. He reached out his hands and placed them round her neck.

She tried to twist the handle. She wanted to scream, but the air was trapped in her throat.

A kick to his shin stunned him briefly enough to loosen his grip sufficiently for her to grapple with the door.

She was out in the fresh air.

'Oh no you don't,' he said. 'Get back in here…'

CHAPTER TWENTY-FOUR

The assembled residents at Downlands Farm had an uninterrupted view towards Flint Cottage. Having shared their perspectives, it came as no surprise to witness events unfolding. They saw the door of the cottage fling open.

'Ursula!' said Stanley as they observed in horror the hands clasped around Ursula's neck.

Together, in a pack, they bolted down. The men hurled themselves upon Quentin, tackling him to the ground. Bridget and Imogen scooped a hysterical Ursula away.

'How could you?' she shouted at Quentin. 'How *could* you?'

Quentin heaved under the weight of the men until eventually he accepted that the struggle was over. Stanley made something of an informal citizen's arrest but insisted that the police be called immediately. And, in due course, they blazed into Littleworth with sirens and blue flashing lights.

The hamlet became a crime scene once more, with this time plastic tape cordoning off a section of land bordering Flint Cottage and Riplingham Barn where an excavation confirmed the now inevitable gruesome conclusion.

'There are still some things that I'm not clear on,' said Bridget to Stanley as he placed his bag in the boot of his car. 'There's part of me that still can't believe it's happened. I can't stop thinking of Ursula. To imagine what she must be going through.'

Stanley closed his boot. 'I think we all fell into the trap of believing that everyone knows everyone else's business in this small place. Whereas, in reality, the truth was hidden from us in plain sight.'

'You say he hid what had happened to poor Skye from both Ursula and his ex-wife? Doesn't that sound unlikely?'

'Not implausible at all,' said Stanley. 'The dysfunctional relationship between the three of them made it easy for Quentin to play one off against the other. It was the distance between Ursula and Nancy that made it possible. Feeding Nancy a narrative that Skye wanted nothing to do with her and that he was still in contact with her. It was only in Ursula going to see Nancy in person that the myths were debunked. She saw that he'd been lying to both of them.'

'Yes, he'd played them off against one another.'

It was Imogen's recollection of what had happened during her work experience at Flint Cottage that had cemented his theory on Quentin's method. She hadn't expected her time there to be so dull. To sit quietly in Ursula's presence as she wrote was hardly what she'd imagined. It was what prompted her in the afternoon, when Quentin went out for his daily constitution, to be proactive. Instead of sitting with Ursula, she made herself busy by tidying some of the paperwork in Quentin's study. She thought she was being helpful. That's why it was such a shock when Quentin returned and raged at her. Accusing her of meddling with things that didn't concern her.

'Imogen didn't realise what she'd seen that day,' said Bridget.

'No,' said Stanley. 'And why should she? To the innocent eye it all looked completely inane. Nothing of any significance.'

'It explains why he refused to move with the time as far as submitting manuscripts was concerned.'

'Exactly. By sending out Ursula's manuscript through the mail and asking a publishing house to return the enclosed sealed and stamped addressed envelope as acknowledgement of receipt, he had a perfect foil. With the birthday card to Ursula within and written in an impersonation of Skye's handwriting, it's easy to see how the deception was made.'

'And Imogen, in trying to be helpful, had filed away the latest envelope to be sent?'

'I believe that's what happened.'

'I can see why he would be afraid. He must've wondered whether Imogen had realised what he was doing. She was certainly shocked by his outburst. Enough to pretend to be ill in order not to return for the remainder of her week with them.'

Bridget could see how the clouds were gathering for him. George's dogged determination to get planning approval for the storytelling huts, and a fear that his lies might be known to Imogen, all added to his growing paranoia.

'We may never know his true psychology,' said Stanley.

'Something of the shadows about him, wouldn't you say?'

'That's a nice way of expressing it.'

It was nearing the end of the day. The sun had dipped on the horizon.

'Do you have to move on so soon?' she asked. 'Won't you stay a little longer?'

His car door was open. 'You don't need me anymore. I think you'll settle things quicker without me around.'

Bridget wasn't sure. She liked what Stanley brought to Littleworth. She'd be forever grateful for the justice he'd brought for George. Although, he wasn't the only one she needed to thank.

'Did you know who your mystery client was?' she asked.

'I had my suspicions.'

Jimbo had made himself known after Bridget's account of her curtailed experience at Flint Cottage. His name was actually Tom James. But everybody called him Jimbo. It was he who had waited at the station for Skye that fateful day. The boy who she'd planned to go travelling with. He'd been disappointed that she hadn't. He'd assumed that she'd got cold feet. But there was always a tiny doubt at the back of his mind. And over time, he wouldn't be the first to wonder how somebody could vanish entirely.

'Would you call it instinct?' asked Bridget.

'Maybe. More likely, when he saw the first reports of a suspicious death in the last place he'd known Skye to have been, he simply wondered *'what if?''*

'Thank goodness he did.'

'He did well to keep himself out of the investigation. Just observing from the sidelines. Only once steering me in a direction by writing me a note inviting me for afternoon tea with Ursula. It was a clever way of getting me into Flint Cottage.'

Bridget saw how almost all the pieces fitted together. What had once looked such a muddle now made entire sense. There was one thing she was still curious about:

'The birthday cake?' she said. 'You were insistent that the birthday cake had brought it all together for you?'

'As I said, I'd narrowed it all down to two significant names: Joyce and Ursula. Will told me that George had said he'd "told her the truth". And this was *before* the cake was brought out. Which meant that he'd not been to see Joyce yet, so he *must've* been referring to Ursula.'

It was all a matter of logic.

'I suppose seeing George in that state, Quentin saw an opportunity.'

'He's not a stranger, as we've seen, to lashing out. Underneath that respectable prim exterior lies quite a temper. The weather that night was in his favour. The crime was surprisingly easy to commit.'

'To think he almost got away with it.'

Stanley got in his car and wound down his window. There was something pensive about his expression. He looked almost wistful.

'There are many crimes that go unaccounted for,' he said. 'Miscarriages of justice do happen. Sometimes the guilty escape justice. Sometimes the innocent are framed. And sometimes crimes are never uncovered at all.' Bridget thought he spoke from the heart. 'In this instance, we can be satisfied that one of the potential injustices have been resolved.'

It was this, she guessed, that spurred him on. This was his fight. More of a crusade, it sounded, than a nine-to-five job.

They heard a little chink of glasses. Zara was collecting the last of the empty glasses from the tables outside The Plough. She gave them both a wave before settling her hand upon her swollen belly as she moved back inside.

Life is full of choices, Stanley thought again.

'It's got me thinking,' ventured Bridget, 'that perhaps I might pick up George's baton and do something about his storytelling huts. I'd have to put my own slant on it. Perhaps more of an educational angle?' She was thinking of her history in the classroom. Of the person she'd once been.

'That sounds like a good idea,' said Stanley. 'I think there might be something in it.'

Bridget felt emboldened by his encouragement. She looked up to Downlands Farm with fresh eyes. The love for her husband and family ran deep. It was funny how one could have ideas about how life was going to play out. To have it all sketched out like a road map. Only to discover that the eventual route bore no resemblance to the draft.

His engine was running now.

They bid each other goodbye. Many things felt unsaid between them. Stanley was a good type of person to talk to. He was the unique type of person who truly listened. She would've liked to have spoken with him a great deal more. As he pulled away, Bridget wondered – a little sadly – whether she'd ever see him again.

The sky had lit up with an extraordinary sunset. It was painted in pink, apricot, purple, red, yellow… In fact, she thought, it was every colour of the rainbow.

She waved at his car as it moved away on the road out of Littleworth, even waving a little longer after it had disappeared from view entirely.

THE END

Printed in Great Britain
by Amazon

16701041R00125